The Pony Whisperer

THE PONY REBELLION

Collect all of the Pony Whisperer books:

The Pony Whisperer

THE PONY REBELLION

JANET RISING

sourcebooks
jabberwocky

Copyright © 2012 by Janet Rising
Cover and internal design © 2012 by Sourcebooks, Inc.
Series design by Liz Demeter/Demeter Design
Cover photography © Mark J. Barrett
Cover images © jentry/iStockphoto.com; ivetavai/iStockphoto.com; lugogarcia/
iStockphoto.com; Kwok Chi Chan/123rf.com; Polina Bobrik/123rf.com;
Alexandr Shebanov/123rf.com; Pavel Konovalov/123rf.com

Published by Sourcebooks Jabberwocky, an imprint of Sourcebooks, Inc.
P.O. Box 4410, Naperville, Illinois 60567-4410
(630) 961-3900
Fax: (630) 961-2168
www.jabberwockykids.com

First published in Great Britain in 2010 by Hodder Children's Books.

Library of Congress Cataloging-in-Publication data is on file with the publisher.

Source of Production: Versa Press, East Peoria, Illinois, USA
Date of Production: April 2012
Run Number: 17447

Printed and bound in the United States of America.
VP 10 9 8 7 6 5 4 3 2 1

To Sue and Tiffany, Karen and Shandycourt, Lesley and Solo, Jan and Moo, Nicky and Bridget, and my mount Libby—the first Havering Park Bareback and Bridleless Musical Ride!

Chapter 1

"OK, come clean, what have you all done wrong?" asked James, running his hand through his dark blond hair so that it stood up on end.

"Nothing," said Katy, "but thanks for the vote of confidence—*not!* Besides, we might ask you the same thing!"

"I feel as though I've done something—even though I know I haven't," sighed Bean. "Er, Pia, what's my feed scoop doing on your hay bales?"

"You left it there," I told her, trying not to look at James. I feel kinda funny whenever he does that thing with his hair, and I was scared someone else would notice. "You're always leaving stuff on my hay."

"Am I? I wondered where that went," Bean mumbled, casually lobbing her scoop back toward her corner of the barn—everyone had a sectioned-off part in the building where they kept their own pony's feed and bedding. The scoop disappeared into the black hole of empty feed sacks, baler twine, and buckets that was Bean's domain. It was easily the messiest part of the barn and so very Bean.

"What did Sophie say to you, Pia?" Katy asked, tying her red hair back behind her head with a band.

"She just said to be in the barn at ten o'clock Saturday

because she had something important to say," I told her, remembering that Sophie had winked when she'd told me, which I had found a little weird.

"Mmmm, that's what she said to me too," Katy said, frowning. "What do you think she's up to?"

"She's late, anyway," remarked James, looking at his watch. "If she's not here in two minutes, I'm going. Anyone want to go riding? I thought I'd take Moth up to Badger's Copse then back through the hillside for a good ride."

"So you're in on whatever it is too, are you?" asked Katy.

"Of course!"

"I'll come riding with you," I told James.

"Mmm, me too," said Katy.

"Count me in," added Bean. "I couldn't ride last night so Tiffany will be fresh. Plus it's cold today, so she'll be even livelier."

It was cold, the sort of dry cold that usually follows a heavy frost. The sun was out, but it was too early in the morning to compete successfully against the chill. Even in the barn I could see my breath hanging in the air like mini clouds as I spoke—but I love frosty mornings. They're so much better than those dank, dark, dismal, drizzly days that put everyone in a bad mood, especially me. It was early November, and the ponies were all clipped and in at night. I thought of Drummer, rugged up and warm in his stable. He was bound to put in a buck or two on our hack before settling down, especially if the other ponies were fresh too. I'd have to keep my knees in and my heels down if I wanted to keep admiring the scenery, rather than sitting in the middle of it.

Suddenly, we heard a car in the drive. Two doors slammed shut.

"At last!" said James, as Dee-Dee and her mom, Sophie, appeared at the barn doorway. "Now maybe we'll find out what the big secret is!"

But Sophie, as usual, was on her cell phone. "Yes, OK," she said, nodding (don't know why, whoever she was talking to couldn't see her). "I'm just about to ask them now. Yes, that's right. No worries. Absolutely. Sure thing. I'll get back to you directly, Linda, and let you know what we'll be doing. Sure. OK…" Dee-Dee looked at all of us and rolled her eyes. I heard James sigh. Well, it was more of a *huff*, really. And then someone I didn't want to see walked through the barn door.

"Hi, Cat!" said Katy. "Are you in on this big mystery as well?"

"What mystery?" Cat asked, her short, dark hair sticking up in that sassy way it does, giving her the sort of air about her that stops you from messing with her. "Sophie just asked me to be here at ten so here I am."

My heart sank. Catriona and I do not get along. Actually, that's an understatement; we don't just not get along, we don't get along in an epic way. In the past, Cat has plotted against me, plotted against Drummer, and wasted no opportunity to diss me in front of anyone passing by. She used to go out with James (which was the best way to get to me—only I'd die if anyone knew that), which means that things are sometimes a bit strained between the two of them now. She's the only negative at Laurel Farm, where I keep Drum. Oh, and she's adamant that I am not a Pony Whisperer—even though I can totally hear what horses and ponies are saying (under one important condition) and everyone else is on board with it. I think that's our relationship in a nutshell. Except that when I went away on a riding trip with Bean in the spring, leaving my beloved Drummer in the capable hands of Katy, it was Cat—through a cruel twist of fate—that ended up looking after him. And, naturally, I then had to thank her when I returned, especially as she'd looked after him really well. Only when I'd thanked her and given her the gift I'd intended to give to Katy, Cat had shrugged her shoulders, just mumbling an OK at me. It had been awkward. Since then we've gone back to avoiding each other.

Sophie finally snapped her cell phone shut and looked around at us all. "Thanks so much for coming," she began, smiling. She was wearing riding clothes and looked very glamorous—something showing people seem to be able to do without effort. "I have a proposition to make to you all."

"Isn't that something to do with grammar?" Bean whispered to me, on planet Bean, as usual.

"That's a preposition," I whispered back. "I think…"

"My friend Linda is manager at the Taversham branch of the Riding for the Disabled Association. You've probably heard of it," Sophie began.

We all nodded. Taversham was about ten miles away from Laurel Farm.

"Well, Linda is putting on an Equine Extravaganza in their indoor school at Christmas to raise funds, and she's asked me to organize an event to be included."

"If Sophie thinks I'm baking cakes or selling programs she's crazier than I thought," James whispered to me under his breath.

"Shhh," I said. I thought Sophie was strange too, but she was strange in a totally horsey way so I forgave her.

"So I thought it would be wonderful for everyone here to take part in a musical activity ride and perform it on the night of the extravaganza," Sophie concluded. "It's for a great cause, it will be so much fun, and I'm sure you'll all get a lot out of it."

I haven't told you everything about Dee-Dee's mom, have I? She isn't the sort of person you say no to, even if you wanted to. She has a show horse called Lester and Dee shows her own pony, dappled gray Dolly Daydream, at all the top shows. Not just for fun—Sophie is dead serious about it, and poor Dee is always having lessons and training when she'd rather be out riding with us. Only Dolly's very expensive so she can't—mainly because we're always flying around the country out of control. As Sophie finished speaking, Dee looked puzzled. "Are you including me?" she asked.

"Yes, of course!" Sophie replied briskly, as though Dee was stupid.

"Who am I going to ride?"

"Dolly of course. Who do you think?"

"Really?" Dee's jaw dropped. "How come?"

"All the practices will be on soft ground in the school, so there should be no problem with her legs," her mother replied. "Honestly, Dee, who else would you ride?"

"It sounds like a great idea," enthused Katy. "But what exactly is an activity ride?"

"It's a musical ride where you'll go over small jumps in different formations. Sort of like the Rockettes but with horses. And more jumps. You get the picture?" Sophie explained. "It's spectacular. I'll give you all a letter explaining it for you to take home and get your parents to sign. They have to be totally on board with you all doing it and agree to the practices as well as the performance. Obviously you won't need one, Dee," she added.

"It sounds really cool!" cried Bean, suddenly enthusiastic.

"You mean I can jump Dolly?" Dee asked incredulously.

"Yes, Dee. They're only tiny ones—bunny hops—just stop pushing me about it!" said Sophie impatiently.

"It's a miracle!" breathed Dee, falling backward on a hay bale in a mock faint, completely flabbergasted.

Dee wasn't the only one who was surprised—I couldn't believe Sophie was being so casual about Dolly either. It was unheard of.

"Count me in," said James. "Just let me know what you want me to do and I'll be there with Moth. The RDA is a fantastic cause, and it sounds like a great thing to do."

"Me too," said Bean. "There's no way Tiffany and me are being left out!"

"Wild horses wouldn't prevent Bluey and me from being in it too!" agreed Katy, bouncing up and down on a feed sack in excitement.

"And me," I said. It sounded like fun—I'd always admired pony performances and wanted to do something like it, and now here was my chance. I felt a tiny flutter of excitement in the pit of my stomach. I pictured Drum and me sailing over jumps in style, bursting through hoops of paper, soaring through jumps of fire. I imagined a packed gallery clapping and cheering us all in admiration. It would be like being on a TV reality show or something. I mean, how fantastic!

"You can definitely include me and Bambi," said Cat enthusiastically.

The flutter of excitement inside me died, plummeting like it had been shot, and I chewed the inside of my cheek. How was that going to work, me and Cat on a team together? Riding together? Practicing together? Oh for goodness' sake, I thought, we could stay at opposite ends of the ride and pretend that the other wasn't there. I was sure that would work.

It had to work. I wasn't going to be the only one not included in Sophie's activity ride—it sounded like too much fun!

CHAPTER 2

NOW YOU'VE WARMED UP I'll put up a few jumps to see how the ponies tackle them. Who wants to lead?" asked Sophie, leaning back against the fence of the outdoor school and looking at us all.

"I will," volunteered James, steering Moth to the outside track and halting. Katy and Bluey slipped in behind them, followed by Cat with Bambi, Bean and Tiffany, Dee and Dolly, and finally, me and Drum, trying to get as far away from Cat as possible.

"What's all this about?" asked Drummer, his black-tipped ears twitching. With his blanket clip, he was two-tone bay—all shiny and smooth on his front half, all mahogany and fluffy on the back.

"It's very exciting," I told him. "We're in training for an activity ride!"

"No need to ask who'll be responsible for all the activity!" snorted Drum.

I had my two-thousand-year-old stone statue of Epona, Celtic goddess of horses, in my jacket pocket, which is how I can hear what Drummer says. Ever since I found the stone statue of a woman sitting sidesaddle on her stone horse, when Drum and I first moved to Laurel Farm, I'd been able to hear what horses and ponies were saying. The only person who knows that Epona takes the credit for me hearing ponies is James—everyone else believes I'm a Pony Whisperer. Well, explaining would be too tricky, and everyone would want Epona, wouldn't they? That's my excuse, and I'm sticking to it.

Sophie manhandled the yard's lightweight jump blocks into the outdoor school in a line of twos, placing a single pole on each pair to make five jumps in a row along the center. They were only a couple feet high, but without wings we had to meet them in the very center of each pole to avoid the ponies running out.

"OK, I want you to go over these individually, then we'll try it as a ride," said Sophie.

James, Katy, and Cat each did well with the line of jumps. Bean's palomino mare Tiffany, however, was sort of scared.

"Five jumps? In a row? You what?" I heard her snort, drawing herself up to look at least a hand bigger than she was.

"I'll just be a minute," explained Bean, who was used to her pony thinking everything was out to get her. She rode Tiffany around the jumps until she settled—a little—then headed for the first one. Tiffany has a unique jumping style where she sticks her head up in the air and hurtles at the fence like it's a power wall. She could get away with this approach under normal circumstances, but with a row of five jumps, Tiffany was almost on top of the second jump as soon as she landed after the first, giving her the perfect opportunity to do two outs—run out and freak out.

"Not quite the idea," said Sophie dryly, putting her hands on her hips.

"She'll be OK, she just needs to get used to it," grinned Bean.

"I hope so, Bean," said Sophie, "because Tiffany has to jump in a rhythm for this to work. Can you practice on your own until she does?"

"Yes, of course," nodded Bean. "I'll get Pia to help me." *Oh thanks*, I thought. Then I realized she wanted me to talk to Tiffany and explain why it was important to jump properly. I could do that, no problem.

We all turned, fascinated, to watch the novelty of Dee and Dolly going along the line of jumps. We'd never seen them get totally off the ground before—Dee had always been banned from doing anything interesting. But beautiful Dolly took it all in her stride.

"Jumps! Wow!" I heard her say, pricking up her ears and cantering toward them. Sophie had bandaged her legs for protection, and Dolly popped neatly over each jump, her swaddled legs a blur of pink wool.

Then it was my turn. As I headed Drummer for the grid of jumps, I heard him chuckle and my heart sank.

"Shall I run out? Shall I refuse? Shall I trot over some, canter over others, and kick another over?" I heard my bay male horse plotting. But he didn't do any of those things. He popped over them like a perfect pro. What a little liar!

I heaved a sigh of relief. I didn't want to end up having to practice something I knew Drum could do in his sleep—if he wanted to. Or, worse, for us to get rejected from the ride before we'd even begun. Showing off in front of Cat came into it too.

"Great!" enthused Sophie. "You're all wonderful—except you, Bean, but you know what you have to do. Now put yourself at the back, and we'll try it as a ride."

That went sort of OK. Drummer got very excited, being the last to go, and Moth, going all out as usual, was over the last jump before Bluey, behind her, had gotten over the first, but we managed it.

"OK, not bad," said Sophie. "We'll come back to the jumping later. Now I want to see how you and the ponies go as a ride. Stay in the order you are and ride around the outside track while I get rid of these jumps."

So we did. I was glad Tiffany and Dolly were between Bambi and Drum. Not only could I see the others from that position, but Drum and Bambi were sort of a thing these days. When we first got here, Bambi hated Drummer, although he (for some unfathomable reason) thought she was the best thing since sugar cubes. Things didn't improve until Drummer found Bambi after she'd been stolen, and ever since then Bambi has warmed to Drum. She's warmed to him to the point of being scorching hot, and now the pair of them are like those annoying couples you see during breaks at school—totally gross! When I see Drum and Bambi nuzzling each other in the field I think, *Ahh, sweet,*

11

but when I'm riding Drummer, and he's supposed to be working, and he starts sidling up to Cat's skewbald mare and being all sappy, I just think it's annoying.

Aaaaanyway, we trotted around behind the others and I thought the different colors of the ponies looked really nice from my vantage point—and was grateful Drum was nowhere near his beloved Bambi. This, I thought, is a great place to be in an activity ride and perfect for someone (like me) who isn't blessed with a superduper memory. I could easily see what I had to do and just follow the others. A weight-off-my-mind moment, definitely.

Unfortunately, Sophie didn't share my thoughts.

"James, you'll have to slow down. You're leaving the others behind," she told him as Bluey struggled to match Moth's stride and the gap between them widened.

James turned in the saddle. "Oh, come on, Moth's barely trying!" he said. Moth rattled on, eating up the ground. A bright chestnut with a white blaze and four white legs, she always went everywhere in a hurry. She was the one pony I never heard speak. Trusting James alone, Moth talks only to him—when he borrows Epona from me as translator.

"Moth always storms along as though her tail's on fire," moaned Cat. Lively Bambi wasn't exactly a limo, horse-wise either, and couldn't keep up with James. Tiffany, on the other hand, had a longer stride.

"I'll go behind James," volunteered Bean, cantering into the gap.

"Oh great," moaned Katy, after another circuit, "now both of you are lapping the rest of us."

It was true. Moth and Tiffany were streaking ahead.

"Mmmm, that won't do," said Sophie, shaking her head. "You two are going to have to slow down. And besides, if you're in second, Bean, you'll be a leader at some point, and Tiffany isn't reliable enough to do that job. Let's try Katy in the lead."

So we did. But that didn't work either. Poor Bluey, Katy's chunky blue roan, held up everyone. The best at jumping cross-country, Bluey's stride was too short to be a leader.

"You'll have to go at the back, Katy," Sophie told her. "You can cut the corners to catch up without hurrying poor Bluey along. Let's try Cat and Bambi in the lead—Pia, you put yourself behind them, then James behind Drummer, Bean behind James as Moth's and Tiffany's strides match and they'll make a good pair, then you, Dee, because you can get Dolly to alter her stride, and finally Bluey. Come on, let's try it trotting!"

"Thank goodness!" I heard Bluey puff. "I thought I was going to pass out there for a minute."

Drummer was thrilled. Trotting along behind Bambi's ample chestnut-and-white backside, I could hear Drummer sigh in contentment. He was thrilled. Thrilled didn't explain how I was feeling. My plan had been to stay well away from Cat, and here I was, thundering along behind her. And what happened to me being able to copy the others?

13

Pooh!

"Now we'll try some simple drill movements!" yelled Sophie. "Whole ride turn up the center from C to A, then split up at A—first left, second right."

That's better, I thought as I turned Drum away from Bambi and we rode along the long side with lots of beautiful nothing in front of us. Maybe I could cope after all.

"Now get level with your partner as you ride along the long side and come up the center again in pairs!" yelled Sophie.

What? My partner? Of course, being second meant I was paired with Cat. My heart sank. This was *so* not turning out as I had anticipated.

We managed it. It's not easy being a pair with someone you're not talking to. *At least there is one blessing*, I thought. Usually, I expected Cat to make snarky comments: with her concentration on the drill riding and with Sophie overseeing us, she was at least mute, rather than rude.

"Oh that's fabulous!" enthused Sophie. "Drum and Bambi make a perfect pair. Their strides match completely. Moth and Tiffany are good together—I knew they would be—and Dee, if you can get Dolly to shorten her stride just a shade more, she and Bluey will match too. Just remember to cut the corners rather than rushing as it looks more professional. Super!"

Was Sophie joking? Drum and Bambi a perfect pair? Did that mean Cat and I were stuck together for the rest of the ride?

Suddenly, this activity ride didn't seem like such a great idea, after all.

"The colors work well too," Sophie continued. "A skewbald and bay in front, Moth and Tiffany look well together being chestnut and palomino—especially with Moth's white legs—and Dolly and Bluey are shades of gray. Perfect! You all look fantastic!"

Cat glanced across at me with a thunderous expression, and I realized that she hated being paired with me just as much as I with her. *Sophie must know how much we don't get along*, I thought. She had to realize how tricky it made things, putting us together.

Cat could bear it no longer. "Are you certain Bambi and Drum should be paired?" she shouted. "I think Drummer's having trouble keeping up with Bambi."

"He most certainly isn't!" I said, angry on Drummer's behalf.

"No, I most certainly am not!" said Drummer testily.

"Yes, yes, you look fabulous together!" enthused Sophie, ignoring her cell phone's ringtone for once. "Now let's try some more movements. As you come up the center line this time and split up, I want you to come across the school from the quarter markers and go across the middle diagonally, one at a time, in the same order you are in single file. Got that?"

I thought so. We came up the center in trot, we split up, we turned diagonally across the school, and I let Catriona and Bambi go first before urging Drummer onto the opposite side, aware that James and Moth were storming along behind Cat and racing us across the middle.

"Slow down, James!" yelled Sophie.

"Hurry up, Pia!" yelled James, reining in Moth.

"You're going too fast!" I yelled back, urging Drummer on. Drummer broke into a canter and sped for the opposite side of the school.

"Slow down, Pia. You're not supposed to canter!" yelled Sophie.

"Who am I supposed to go in front of?" asked Bean.

"Me!" shouted Dee. "Hurry up!"

"Slow down, Bluey can't go that fast!" complained Katy as her blue roan scuttled along, puffing.

"Stop, stop!" shouted Sophie, rather unnecessarily as Tiffany, Dolly, and Bluey formed a pileup in the center.

"Is everyone supposed to be just milling around?" asked Drummer, and we pulled up.

I leaned forward and patted his bay neck. "No, we're not," I explained. "We haven't got the hang of it yet."

"Yet? You're optimistic," I heard him murmur.

"You have to keep your heads on straight," instructed Sophie, "and look at what everyone else is doing so you can adjust your own pony's stride. You need to ride without looking at your pony, but at everyone else so you know where they are and where you're supposed to be next. Don't worry, though, these things are always a mess at the start. You'll soon get the hang of it after a few practices."

"Are you sure?" said Bean doubtfully.

"Positive!" said Sophie firmly. "You'll soon be flying over the jumps in formation. I promise you! Now let's try again."

"What does she mean, a few practices?" asked Drummer.

"We need to practice—we're going to perform at an Equine Extravaganza," I told him.

"How many is 'a few'?"

"Don't start," I said, my heart sinking.

"No, really, how many? Three? Four? More than four?"

"A lot more than four," I told him.

"Hummph!" snorted Drummer, shaking his head.

"Now I want to try another formation…" Sophie said, rearranging the jumps so that instead of a line of five up the center, she had four in the center arranged with each jump at right angles to the next like a big X, and designed to be jumped from quarter marker to quarter marker. Luckily, the poles were made of hollow plastic, so they were easy to move around.

"OK, now as you come across from the quarter markers I want you to jump over these—keep to the left-hand one—in the same order as you did when they weren't there, so Cat jumps first, then Pia, followed by James, Bean, Dee, and Katy. You need to keep straight and get your timing right. Up for it?"

We all nodded, getting ourselves into position—and it seemed to work well. Drum flew over our jump just before Moth crossed over behind us, with Bean close on our heels. It was actually starting to feel like fun!

"OK, now I want you to tackle the cross jumps in

pairs, so everyone needs to ride around on the left rein in pairs. Ready?"

We were. I was on the inside, which meant Drummer had to do fairy steps as we cornered while Bambi kept wiggling around. Cat and I still weren't communicating, but as both of us were determined not to give the other anything to complain about, we both made sure we kept in step. I could hear James and Bean having a loud argument behind us—James was accusing Bean of going too slow and Bean was telling him not to be so bossy. Perhaps Cat and I, with our silence is golden policy, had it pretty good after all.

The ponies got a little competitive in their pairs and flew over the jumps with Moth and Tiffany both trying to get ahead of the other, which meant they were breathing down our necks. Sophie scolded James and Bean a little bit, but praised everyone else. We tried it on both reins, and it was really good. I found that I was riding Drummer without thinking about it. Instead, I was looking around and making sure I was level with Cat, and in line for the jumps, and my riding became more instinctive. Asking Drummer to lengthen and shorten his stride to keep with Bambi and get away from Moth and Tiffany behind us made me concentrate more too, and I couldn't hear the ponies moaning as much as usual because they had so many instructions from their riders. This activity ride was improving our riding—which was an added bonus.

"OK, that's wonderful!" cheered Sophie as we all came to a halt. The ponies were puffing a bit—and so were we.

"I think you've all done really well. You look like an activity ride already!" Sophie continued. "We'll call it a day. Can you all make tomorrow for another practice? And then Monday after school, say five o'clock?"

Everyone could.

"What? More of this?" asked Drummer, still puffing.

"Yes, isn't it great?" I told him, patting his neck.

"Hummph!" Drummer snorted again.

"What's this all about?" I heard Bambi ask him.

"It seems to be an ongoing thing," I heard Drummer reply. "More activity planned for Tuesday, can you believe it?"

"Oh well," Bambi sighed, sidling up to Drummer, "at least we'll be together."

Snatching the reins out of my hands, Drummer leaned over and nuzzled Bambi's neck. "Mmmmm," I heard him murmur, "there is that to it!"

Bambi giggled. I know. Giggled!

I let out a sigh. Looking up, I could see Cat giving me an evil look from Bambi's saddle. I looked away again. How on earth were we going to get through this activity ride if we had to continue riding as a pair? It wasn't possible.

As if she could read my mind, I heard Sophie start talking about how our ride would be helping everyone at Taversham. Well, I thought, if that wasn't an incentive to knuckle down and get on with the ride, I didn't know what was. I could do this! Hostilities could be put aside for this one ride, surely?

The problem was, I didn't know whether Cat felt the same way.

Chapter 3

"Something is going on," I told Bean.

"What do you mean?"

"Well, usually I can't get Mom to shut up whenever she gets a new boyfriend—or boyfriends, plural," I said. "But this time she's being very secretive."

"How so?"

"Just sort of quiet when she reads texts, and not reading her emails when I'm around and not jabbering on about her new boyfriend—or boyfriends—being this and that and Mr. Wonderful, like they all are when they start out and, oh, I don't know, sort of weird."

"Can you have a talk with Tiff before I tackle this line of jumps?" Bean asked me.

We were in the outdoor school, trying to get Tiffany used to the jumps for the activity ride—as promised. I explained to Bean's palomino mare all about it—how she needed to take the jumps steadily, not running out. "They're only tiny jumps, Tiff," I said, "hardly worth getting all worked up for."

"You want me to go over them like everyone else does?" Tiffany asked.

"Yes, that's it. Just for the ride. Can you?"

"I'll try."

I told Bean. "You could have told her that. She can hear you," I said.

"Yes, but it's just a one-way thing when I do it," she pointed out. "No opportunity for feedback."

Bean headed for the jumps and Tiffany did her best. It was better. It wasn't fantastic but an improvement.

"How's that?" Tiffany asked.

"Fantastic!" I lied. "Can you do it even better than that?"

She could, it turned out. Bean was ecstatic and gave her pony a hug.

"You are the smartest pony *ever*!" she told her, wrapping her arms around her golden neck and planting a kiss on her pony's nose where the noseband would have been if it hadn't been taken off due to Tiffany's noseband phobia.

"That's sorted that out, then," I said. "Job done—way to go, Tiff!"

"Maybe he's married," suggested Bean.

"Who?" I said, used to Bean's way of starting a conversation in the middle. As it happens, she wasn't starting a new one but continuing an old one.

"Your mom's new boyfriend."

"That," I declared gloomily, "would be just the end."

"Or he could be hideously disfigured—like in *Beauty and the Beast* or *Phantom of the Opera*."

"Er, do you think?" I asked, frowning.

"Or, maybe he's famous!" Bean was off on one now, totally going for it. "He could be a film star or a singer or royalty! Or a politician—his relationship with your mom could bring down the government! Or, or…"

"Stop!" I said.

"But it is a possibility, isn't it?"

"No. Stop right now. Maybe my mom's realized that there are better ways of handling her relationships. Maybe she's decided to stop embarrassing her only daughter and lie low. I hope so, anyway."

I did too. With all my heart. How wonderful would that be? My mom being all grown-up and sensible and discreet instead of conducting her romances via Facebook and discarding boyfriends like old socks. Bliss! She'd been dating ever since we'd moved to our tiny house—after my mom and dad divorced—and she was still out there, looking for love. I thought it unlikely she was toning things down.

"If you say so," said Bean huffily. "I like my theories better. I bet she's got some famous big shot wrapped around her finger and has had to sign the official secrets act or whatever it is."

"I'm sure you don't have to do that just if you're going out with someone," I said doubtfully.

"I bet you do. I bet you do if you're seeing a prince—or a *spy*. I bet that's it, she's seeing a spy! And maybe"—Bean's eyes narrowed and she prodded my arm with her finger like it was my fault—"he's an enemy spy. That's why she's keeping it under wraps! Or—oh I know, I *know*, your mom's a spy! Has she been sidling up to people in raincoats in parks with briefcases and starting conversation with *The snow is beautiful in Moscow this time of year* or *Red Squirrel flies tonight?"*

"No," I said, without bothering to even try to remember.

"She wants to be careful. She could end up in Alcatraz waiting to be tried for treason."

"Well, it's been great talking this through with you, Bean," I told her sarcastically. "I feel much better about it now."

"I would hate for you to get a nasty surprise," Bean said darkly.

"Too bad you didn't think of that before—it's too late now," I replied dryly, all Bean's possibilities swimming around my head like piranhas in a tank.

When I got home, Mom was still acting weird.

"What are you doing?" I asked her as I walked into the sitting room to see her hastily gathering up a mountain of brown paper in her arms.

"Er, nothing. Just tidying up. What would you like for dinner?"

She'd tried the dinner diversion on me before when I'd spotted her shopping online. I was sure the brown paper contained a vital clue to her weird behavior.

"What's that?" I asked, peering at it and thinking it was very plain, like it was disguised.

"Just some trash," she replied, a bit too innocently. "I'll put it in the recycling." Only she didn't, she hid it away upstairs.

Could she be a spy? No, I shook my head. Bean had gotten under my skin—I'd be as crazy as she was in no time if I listened to her. It was living with her artistic mom, dad, and two gifted sisters that did it, I decided—too much creativity around. *Get a grip, Pia*, I told myself. Mom's a grown-up and entitled to have a few secrets of her own, isn't she? I mean, what would spies buy off the Internet? Bugging devices? Code books? Maybe the plain package was a disguise for my mom. Would I recognize her in the future? Could it be kinky stuff? Oh please no! Kinky stuff came in brown paper, didn't it?

"Mom," I began when she came back downstairs and started rummaging in the fridge. "Mom, what's going on?"

"Going on?" she asked, ever so casually. "I don't know what you mean."

"You'd tell me if there was something," I continued, "right?"

"Of course, why wouldn't I?" It was still a bit casual for my liking, as though she'd been expecting me to ask and had thought out all the answers beforehand. Like a spy would. The thought sprang into my mind uninvited and unwanted. Bean really had gotten me going! I decided to bite the bullet and ask her.

"Er, Mom, your love life has been a bit quiet lately—any new boyfriends on the horizon you haven't told me about?"

"Um, I didn't think you were that interested," she replied rather casually, her head still in the fridge.

I was sure we didn't have so much in there to keep her enthralled for that long. Suspicious! "Oh, I like to keep up with developments," I said, equally casually.

"Er, well, yes, I have actually," she said.

"What's he like, then?" I asked.

"Oh, you know, the usual," she replied. "Want some hot dogs? We can have them with french fries," she said, holding up a packet of Big-n-Beefy Dogs temptingly.

Who was she kidding? There was no "usual" with my mom. Just weirdos—different, geeky weirdos. I wasn't giving up.

"What's his name?"

"Name? Michael. Mike. Hot dogs then?"

"OK," I agreed. "What's he like?"

"Er, well, he's very nice. He, um, rides a bike."

Ahhh, I thought, *the plot thickens.* I could be a spy at this rate. A vision flashed before me. A vision of geeky Michael on a bicycle, pedaling like crazy. Big, bulging thighs wider than my waist, a cycle helmet jammed onto his head. Determined expression. Thin. Very thin. Extra thin like a flat cracker, with bumps where his elbows, hips, and knees were. Covered in bright yellow and black Lycra, like a wasp (not that wasps wear Lycra, but you know what I mean). One of those sporty types who couldn't sit still. Sort of red in the face. I shuddered and felt a bit better. Mike sounded exactly like the type of guy my mom would have a date with. No change there. I sighed. I'd been worried about nothing. Maybe. Or had Mom invented Mike to draw me off the scent? Was Mike a foil so she could carry on her illicit activities, whatever they were?

You can't pull the wool over this girl's eyes, I thought, vowing to stay on my guard.

"Pia, love, can you call your dad? He called earlier to talk to you," my mom-who-may-or-may-not-be-a-spy said.

"OK." I went upstairs and speed-dialed Dad's number on my cell phone, and we chatted for a while about school and stuff. Then I told him all about the activity ride and how exciting it was. He wanted to know when it was going to be performed so I told him—and all about the Equine Extravaganza. "That sounds wonderful, Pumpkin!" he boomed down the phone.

"Er, Dad, can you not call me that, please?" I pleaded. I thought I'd cracked that one, but he had relapses now and again. I hate being called Pumpkin. It would be under-standable if I were big, fat, and orange, but I'm not!

"It's just a little pet name," he replied soothingly.

"Lyn and I have pet names for each other…" He yelled away from the phone, "Don't we, Fluffball?"

Fluffball? *More like Furball*, I thought, remembering how I'd caught stable cat Twiddles Scissor-Paws gagging on his own personal furball on one of Drummer's bales of straw. I mean, Skinny made me gag. She was the reason my dad had left home and my parents divorced.

"Well, anyway," I continued, desperate not to know the ins and outs of my dad's and Skinny Lynny's personal lives, "that's what I've been doing, Dad."

"Well, Lyn and I will be there to watch your little ride," Dad said decisively. "We enjoyed seeing you at Hickstead, and this sounds like a great night out. Will there be a bar?"

How would I know? "Dunno," I said, my heart sinking. I should have known they'd want to come and watch. I didn't relish the prospect. Things were never very comfortable whenever Mom was in the same vicinity as Dad and his younger girlfriend. Me and my big mouth. And I hoped there wasn't going to be a bar because I was still traumatized by my mom's encounter with several glasses of wine when I went on TV. So not a happy memory. My heart sank even lower as a dark cloud of gloom settled over me and threatened to stay there until after the activity ride had been performed. "Your little ride," my dad had called it. Jeez! *Still*, I thought, brightening up, *Dad will probably forget.*

Skinny wanted a word. When I'd been to stay with Dad, I'd actually managed to sort of get along with her. When she wasn't with Dad, she didn't play the little girl lost and was bearable. With Dad in the background she reverted to type.

"Hello, Pia!" she gasped in her little girl voice (see what I mean). "How's Drummer?"

"He's fine, thanks," I said, appreciating her effort to take an interest. She and Drummer didn't get along. Surprise!

"What would you like for Christmas?"

"Oh." Didn't see that one coming. "Can I think about it?" I asked her.

"Of course!" she said. "If you like, we can go shopping again and you can pick out some clothes. That was fun last time, wasn't it?"

Ditto that. I'd got some designer stuff and Skinny (or

rather, my dad) had paid. Awesome! That sounded like a good plan to me and worth giving up a morning for. I nodded enthusiastically, then realized she couldn't see me.

"That would be fantastic, thanks," I croaked, feeling a bit guilty at how quickly I'd sold out for the promise of some new gear. Still, I told myself, I was continuing to work on my relationship with Skinny so shopping together could only help.

"Good!" said Skinny. "We'll organize a date before the stores get too crowded. Here's Paul again. See you later!"

"Yeah, right, OK," I replied.

"OK, Pump—I mean, Pia," remembered Dad, miracle! "Glad you're having fun with Drummer, and we'll arrange that shopping date very soon! Oh," he added, just before I hung up, "say hello to your mother for me, will you? And get two tickets for your little riding thingy, I mean it—I'll send a check to cover the cost, just fill in the amount!"

So much for my dad forgetting.

CHAPTER 4

"Now we need to practice some of the more compli-cated movements," said Sophie, "because if you can't do them, I'll need to rethink everything."

We all nodded silently, as we lined up in the middle of the school on the ponies after our warm-up. The floodlights shone down on us like we were celebrity football players. I was sandwiched between Katy and James on this crisp Monday evening after school, and we had our first audi-ence. Leanne and Mrs. Bradley were sitting on the bench outside the fence, giving us the eye. Leanne, who only ever does competitions on her dun pony, Mr. Higgins, man-aged to look both superior and curious; and ancient Mrs. Bradley, who owns temperamental Henry, the black Dales pony, was already in awe, looking both impressed and ex-cited. You had to like her—she was a sweet old thing even if she did let Henry do exactly what he liked. Combined, the pair of them were an accident waiting to happen disguised as a fluffy black pony and a cute old lady. My thoughts flew unbidden back to my mom. If she disguised herself as an old lady, would I recognize her? Could she, even now, actually be Mrs. Bradley, looking so innocent under the floodlights?

Get a grip, Pia, and concentrate, I told myself. I had no

idea what the more complicated movements were, but was confident we could all do them. How complicated could they be? I was about to find out.

"OK," said Sophie, switching off her cell phone (which gave me the first pang of misgiving), "let's go. Tie your reins in a knot so that they don't dangle around your ponies' legs when you let go of them."

Bean and I exchanged glances. *What did she mean*, I thought, *let go of our reins?* Surely I didn't hear that right.

"Now can you all bring your right leg over the back of the saddle and stand up on your left stirrup—as though you were getting off."

"But we're supposed to take both feet out of the stirrups when we dismount," Katy pointed out.

"I know that, Katy, but imagine you were getting off cowboy style," Sophie suggested.

We all swung our legs over and stood up on the left stirrup. Bean disappeared under Tiffany's stomach as Tiffany, wearing her saddle in an off the shoulder manner, dived out of line.

"Sorry," puffed Bean, picking herself up off the sand and running after Tiffany. "Forgot to tighten my girth!"

"You don't really need me to check all your tack before we start like this is some beginners' lesson, do you?" Sophie asked, annoyed.

"No, sorry, it won't happen again," Bean assured her, turning red and saddling Tiffany who looked completely spooked. Mind you, she always looks like that.

"OK," said Sophie, "the rest of you can sit back again. Now can you all take your jackets off?"

"While we're on board?" asked Bean, not unreasonably. Usually, taking off items of clothing while still in the saddle wasn't the best idea in case your pony—any pony—got scared.

"I'll hold Tiffany's head," offered Sophie, taking the palomino's bridle as Bean looked doubtful. "I assume the bridle's on tight?"

I struggled out of my quilted jacket. Drummer just sighed with boredom. Tiffany's head flew up and darted from side to side as Bean struggled out of her jacket, but she didn't go anywhere. She seemed to be getting used to the strange demands—and besides, she didn't dare do anything with Sophie hanging on to her. We all sat with our jackets dangling by our sides, shivering in the cold.

"Great!" enthused Sophie. "Now put them on again. Bean, you're going to have to practice a lot to get Tiffany totally bored with it."

Bean nodded.

"Let's try it trotting around the outside," Sophie suggested.

"Try what?" asked Cat.

"We'll start by going over onto one stirrup," said Sophie, like it was something simple.

"At trot?" gulped Katy.

"No problem!" James said.

"Can't we start walking?" I asked, not convinced I could

do it. These complicated movements were more complicated than I'd envisaged.

"No, trotting is best, Pia—it will push you more, and you'll find it easier," Sophie said. "Just remember to keep your left knee bent, hold on to the mane, and go for it! The more you act nervous, the harder it will be."

We all made our way onto the outside track in our usual order on the left rein, with Drummer and me behind Cat and Bambi, and set off around the school in trot. Once Cat had established a steady rhythm, Sophie instructed us all to go over onto our left stirrup.

I went for it, as instructed, keeping my left knee bent so that it absorbed the bouncing of Drummer's stride.

"Keep trotting!" ordered Sophie.

Ignoring her, Bluey stopped, convinced that Katy wanted off. Moth overtook me in a canter with James effortlessly standing on one side of her—he was annoyingly good at it, probably because he'd done lots of gymkhana games—and Tiffany darted forward into the space they'd left, shoving her nose into Drummer's tail in an effort to bury herself in denial. I could see Drummer's ears waggling about in confusion, but he obediently kept trotting after Bambi. Cat was doing it perfectly. *She would*, I thought.

"OK, some of you are wonderful, the others need some work," said Sophie. "Let's try again."

We spent the next half hour balancing on one leg at trot, and the ponies soon picked it up. Then we dropped our reins and took off our jackets—with no dead bodies to report. As long as Bambi kept trotting, the others fell in behind and got the idea and even Tiffany settled down. I was amazed. So was Drummer. "What are you doing up there?" he asked me. "Can't you keep still?"

"This is what we're supposed to be doing. It's what the activity ride is all about," I told him. "It's the activity part!"

I heard him sigh. He and the other ponies obviously thought we'd lost it completely.

"It looks pretty boring from down here," he remarked.

"OK, let's try it jumping," said Sophie, putting up the jumps.

"What!" yelled Bean.

"Oh yes, you'll not only be jumping in formation, but you'll be jumping with your arms outstretched, taking off your jackets, and coming over onto one stirrup. Didn't I tell you?"

"She knows she didn't!" Bean muttered to me.

"I think this is going to be fun!" said Katy, confident now she could do it trotting.

"She must be joking!" I heard Cat grumble.

"It's totally going to rock!" cheered James.

I agreed—but only if we didn't fall off.

With the jumps in place, we all followed Cat around the school and up the center line, five jumps away from disaster.

Bambi popped neatly over the first one, and Cat came over onto her left stirrup like a pro. As Drummer landed from the first jump and headed to the second, I grabbed the middle of his mane and tried it—and it worked. It actually wasn't as hard as I'd thought, providing I kept my knee bent and looked forward—and providing Drummer went straight, which he did. By the time we reached the last jump, I was back in the saddle and able to steer Drummer in the opposite direction to Bambi so I could watch James make easy work of it on Moth. Bean's confidence, however, deserted her, and although she kicked her right foot out of her stirrup, she couldn't bring herself to throw her leg over Tiffany's quarters. Dee, used to doing what her mom told her, made it look easy, and Katy looked like she'd been doing it for all her life.

"I always wanted to be in the circus!" James yelled.

Leanne and Mrs. Bradley clapped from the sidelines.

"See, it wasn't as hard as you all thought, was it?" beamed Sophie. "Apart from you, Bean. You just have to believe you can do it!"

"Yes, honestly, Bean, it's not so hard if you just go for it!" Katy told her.

"Oh really?" Bean replied, coming around for another try.

"Great!" yelled Katy as Bean threw her right leg over Tiffany's rump over the first jump.

"Terrible!" yelled James as Bean overbalanced and landed on the floor on her backside.

"Ouch!" she cried. "Can someone catch Tiffany?"

"Are you all right?" asked Sophie, helping Bean up. "I don't remember asking you to dismount!"

We tried again and this time Bean managed it. She also managed a huge grin.

"Easy!" she yelled, punching the air. More clapping from our small audience in the corner.

We tried it again, taking our coats off this time—and we had to be quick because five jumps come at you pretty fast. After a couple of attempts, our coats were all off by the third jump—then we came around and over the jumps for a second time and put them on again.

Tiffany was being amazingly good. She seemed to take confidence from being behind Moth and Drummer, so it was a good thing she wasn't a leader, after all.

After that, jumping with our arms outstretched was a piece of cake.

"Phew," Dee-Dee said, when we took five, "if you'd told me by the end of the morning I'd be able to jump hanging off one side of Dolly, with my arms outstretched and getting undressed, I'd have said you were crazy, but it isn't so hard, after all."

"As long as we don't have to do all three at once!" laughed Katy.

"Do you think we could…?" James asked.

"Don't be ridiculous, James!" Bean yelled, pushing herself back in the saddle after landing on Tiffany's neck over the last jump.

"How's Dolly doing?" I asked Dee.

"Great!" she said. "And it's so fantastic to be doing something fun for a change, instead of never-ending circles around a show ring. It's terrific!"

"You're amazing leaders, you and Pia," I heard Katy

tell Cat. "I'd hate to be the ones who have to think about where to go. I'd much rather follow."

Hmmmm, I thought. That's what I'd hoped to do.

"Bambi's got a great rhythm once she gets going," Cat said. "I just put her into gear and off she goes."

That is weird, I thought. For once, Cat hadn't said anything hateful about me. It couldn't last.

"OK, team," said Sophie, "let's try something else while you're all on a high. I want us to end the ride in a spectacular way. Dee, bring Dolly over here and I'll get you to show everyone. It's only fair I try it out on my own offspring before anyone else tries it."

Dee steered Dolly to the middle of the school and Sophie held on to the dappled gray mare's bridle.

"OK, now swing your left leg over Dolly's neck so that both legs are on the off side." Dee did as she was instructed, pulling a face of mock terror at us all.

"Now grab hold of the pommel and cantle, front and back of your saddle...that's right...now lean back and bring your legs up and over..."

I watched in amazement as Dee's head went down toward her empty left stirrup and her legs folded up over the saddle, over her head and down to the ground in a backward somersault on Dolly's left-hand side. Dolly never flinched.

"And let go of the saddle when you're almost there... great! One perfect backward roll, well done! Now who wants to try next?"

"Oof," said Dee, clutching her head. "That makes you sort of dizzy."

"What's it like, Dee?" asked Bean, looking doubtful.

"OK, actually!" Dee grinned and patted Dolly's dappled neck.

Sophie held each pony in turn and helped us with our backward roll. It was the weirdest sensation as I got my legs to go up and over—and Drummer just sighed and looked bored.

"If you're going to be dismounting like this in the future, perhaps you'd let me know," he said.

"Don't forget to let go of the saddle, Pia, before your legs hit the ground," Sophie reminded me a bit too late. My arms got pulled almost out of their sockets.

"Right, now we have all the basics sorted out, we need to put together a routine. We need some helpers on the ground…" She turned to our audience. "Would you consider helping us?" she asked.

"Oh, I'd love to help!" cried Mrs. Bradley, her eyes lighting up.

Nah, I told myself, no way could that be my mom in disguise. She'd have had a fit if she'd seen me attempt a backward roll off Drummer. Either that or she was very, very good at being a spy.

"Er, OK, if you like," agreed Leanne, almost keeping the boredom out of her voice. I told you Sophie was impossible to say no to. Leanne never wanted to do anything with any of us.

"We really need two more helpers—do any of you know anyone?"

"I bet Dec will do it—won't he, Cat?" said James.

"Yeah, he'll be up for it," Cat agreed, nodding. Declan was one of her brothers and one of James's friends.

"What would we have to do, exactly?" asked Mrs. Bradley.

"Oh, just move the jumps around as the ride develops and hold on to a broom handle or two," Sophie said airily.

"Broom handles?" asked James. "Explain!"

Sophie laughed. "All in good time," she said mysteriously, "but you'll all love it, I promise!"

CHAPTER 5

"TIFFANY IS DEFINITELY GETTING braver, don't you think?" asked Bean as her golden mare demonstrated her courage by snorting and sidestepping a puddle.

"No," James and I said together.

"Well, I think she is," Bean said defensively, shrugging her shoulders.

"She's better on the activity ride than I thought she'd be, I have to admit that," James said.

"Mmmm, that's true," I agreed.

The three of us were making our way back to Laurel Farm having enjoyed a fantastic ride around the countryside in the fall sunshine. All the leaves still clinging to the trees were burnished fiery red and gold by the afternoon sunlight, and the ponies' hooves made a swishing sound as they walked through the crisp leaves that had already fallen. I could hear Drummer and Tiffany muttering away to each other and, occasionally, I even heard Moth add a whisper to the equine conversation. This was progress—she still didn't speak directly to me—but at least she was getting confident enough to converse with the other ponies when she knew I could hear her. But only just.

"Moth needs clipping again. Her coat has grown so fast,"

I remarked, looking at the sweat on Moth's chestnut neck, making her half-grown coat crinkle up like a wet sheep.

James nodded. "I know. I'll ask Sophie whether she'll have time next week when I'm at school. Oh, I forgot to tell her, Dec's totally up for helping out with the activity ride—moving jumps and stuff. I sort of twisted his arm."

I sniffed, wondering whether Declan would be as anti Pia as his sister.

"He helped you when you rescued Moth, didn't he?" asked Bean, sitting another swerve from Tiffany around something that couldn't be seen by the naked eye and probably wasn't there.

"Yup, he's a good friend," confirmed James. "And he's really into working out. He'll be perfect for running around and moving things. Hey, what's going on?" he continued as all the ponies lifted their heads and stared at a man getting out of his car. The bridle path ran alongside a gravel parking lot where people often parked while they walked their dogs, but this man was alone and dressed in a suit—not usual garb for a hike around the countryside. He beckoned us over, clearly reluctant to walk far in his expensive shoes.

"Did you lose a horse?" he asked, pushing his glasses up his nose and shivering. He was about Mom's age and managed to look both annoyed and worried at the same time.

James shook his head. "Nope, all present and correct!"

"Well, there's a black horse on the baseball field," continued the man, pointing behind him. "A magnificent black horse wearing a fancy bridle. It isn't supposed to be there you know. The field is sacred, and a horse like that can do a lot of damage. You'll have to remove it."

Bean and I exchanged glances. We didn't care about the baseball field, but a magnificent black horse sounded like news. Wearing a fancy bridle, eh? Lead us to it!

"It's not ours," explained James, "and it doesn't sound familiar. A black horse, you say?"

"Yes, yes," nodded the man, like we were stupid. "A magnificent big black horse," he continued, waving his arms at the magnificence of it all. "On the baseball field, tearing up the grass. You must know who it belongs to."

"Why should we?" asked Bean.

The man turned and looked at her. "You're on horses," he said illogically. Like we know who owns every equine in the vicinity. There are tons of stables around, but we didn't know everyone. It didn't seem worth explaining that.

"We'll take a look if you like," said James, turning Moth in the direction of the community baseball field and pavilion. "We might recognize it." The field was located at the back of the ponies' turnout field, bordered by a lane we could easily get to by a detour.

Satisfied that he'd shifted the burden of ensuring the community baseball field was returned to its original condition, namely horseless, the man shivered again and got back into his car, muttering.

"Let's go see this magnificent black beast!" said James, urging Moth into a trot. Bean and I hustled Tiff and Drummer along behind him.

"Why the hurry?" asked Drummer.

"This mystery black horse sounds exciting!" I told him. "It could be a Friesian, the royal horse of the Netherlands—"

"Or there might be a reward!" interrupted Bean, over-hearing me, "if he's really that important."

"I wonder if we could sneak a ride on it," James said. "It might be our only chance to ride a circus horse, or an escaped competition horse or film horse!"

I felt my heart thumping in my chest. This was an adventure!

As we drew nearer to the baseball field we slowed the ponies so as not to frighten the magnificent mystery horse. However, we all wanted to be the first to see it, and we crammed three abreast along the track (I ignored Drummer's protests) in a hurried walk. The bushes obscured our view until we turned past the last one and eagerly craned our necks to catch our first glimpse of the magnificent black horse in its fancy bridle.

So-called.

"Somebody is playing a trick on us," wailed Bean. "Honestly, this has to be right up there for anticlimax-of-the-year award!"

"Some magnificent black horse!" I said, my shoulders sagging along with my expectations.

"Ugly black horse, more like," added James.

We stared at the horse that had received top billing. It lifted its head and stared back, still chewing the hallowed grass.

"Well, give me a hat and call me Charlie, what's he doing here?" I heard Drummer say. Then he shouted—only James and Bean heard a neigh whereas I heard, "Hey, Henry, you dumb old hillbilly, what are you doing here? Practicing for the World Series? Ha, ha!"

Mrs. Bradley's pushy Dales pony neighed back something about making a hole in the field hedge and finding some tasty new grass.

"Call that a fancy bridle?" asked Bean, disgusted. "It's Henry's tattered old blue head collar. Somebody needs glasses."

"He was wearing glasses," I said, gloomily.

"Well, he should've gone to LensCrafters," said Bean.

Nobody laughed.

"Good thing we checked him out," James said, dismounting and diving under the single rail boundary to the baseball field after handing Moth's reins to me. "I'll go and catch him."

We watched as James walked up to Henry, but Henry was having none of it. I heard him say, "Get lost!" as James approached him, then he whirled around and trotted off to the far end, near the pavilion. He also lifted his tail and left further evidence of his presence alongside his hoofprints. I wondered what Mr. (shortsighted or possibly crazy) Pinstripe Man would say when he saw that.

"Come on, James!" I shouted, giggling. "Call yourself a horseman?"

"Want to try?" James yelled back unhappily.

"We couldn't do much worse," Bean sniffed as Henry took off again, shaking his head and snorting as he did so.

Drummer sighed. "I guess no one's in a hurry," he murmured.

"What's that?" Tiffany asked, staring intently at a twig on the ground.

"A twig on the ground," explained Drummer.

"Oh, OK. If you're sure," sighed Tiffany.

Eventually Henry, finding himself cornered, gave himself up and came quietly, allowing James to lead him over to us.

"Now what?" I asked, eyeing up the boundary rails.

"He must have jumped in here. He can jump out again," said James grimly. "Can you take one of my stirrup leathers off Moth's saddle? It'll have to do as a rein."

Dismounting, I wrestled one of James's leathers from Moth's saddle (which wasn't easy as he hardly ever cleans his tack) and threw it over the rail.

With the leather fastened to Henry's head collar as makeshift, very short reins, James jumped onto Henry's unclipped, fluffy black back.

"Come on, you big lump," said James, turning the Dales pony around to run up. "Let's go!"

But Henry didn't want to go. Henry decided to adopt a slo-mo attitude and went at a snail's pace, despite James urging him on with his legs.

"This pony is very badly trained!" his substitute rider grumbled. Mrs. Bradley was quite content to let her dear

Henry wander the countryside at a mile a week, and Henry had become used to dictating the pace. He wasn't about to relinquish control to James.

"*Let's go!*" James yelled angrily, flapping his elbows and kicking Henry's sides. Unused to such positive riding, Henry bounded, surprised, into a canter. Unfortunately, it surprised Tiffany too, and she turned and fled back down the bridle path with Bean clinging on like a leech, having had plenty of practice sitting through her pony's one-eighty turns. Luckily, this gave Henry the idea, and he sailed over the rail after Tiffany with James clinging to his mane. Unluckily, the idea petered out on the other side, and he came to an immediate and very abrupt halt the moment he touched down.

There was a dull thud accompanied by several words I hadn't heard since my dad was cut off on the highway by a maniac in a BMW.

"Are you all right?" I asked, peering down at James. James peered back up at me from under Henry's neck.

"Physically, yes," he said. "Psychologically, no!" He grinned, hauling himself up and brushing leaves off his riding pants. "Where's Bean?"

"Tiffany thought you were talking to her."

"I'm back," said a voice as Bean steered a bug-eyed Tiffany through the trees.

"Where did you get out?" Drummer asked Henry.

"Behind the field shelter—there's a nice big hole there now. I'll show you later," he replied.

"Oh no, you won't!" I said, pulling out my cell phone and speed-dialing Katy.

"What did you say that for?" asked Drummer.

"You asked me!" replied Henry.

"Yeah, well sometimes I think I'll wake up and discover this pony-whispering girl was just a bad dream," I heard Drummer mumbling to himself.

With Katy dispatched to fill in the escape tunnel, we turned for home, James leading Henry from Moth, his spare stirrup dangling from my hand. Henry still wasn't playing ball. He snatched at the hedges, he dawdled, he shook his head trying to get James to drop the makeshift lead rein. In all, he was *so annoying*. Moth didn't look too happy either, and Bean and I found ourselves trying to push the magnificent black horse along in front of us.

"How does Mrs. Bradley put up with this little punk?" James asked, tugging on the stirrup leather.

"She loves him," sighed Bean as though that was all that mattered.

"Hummph!" snorted James, unimpressed.

"I'll take him for a while if you want," I offered. "You'll be better at coaxing him along than I am."

Steering Drummer around Henry, I took the stirrup leather from James, and we proceeded for a while with James successfully shoving Henry along so that he walked beside me.

We reached the path—the quickest way back to the yard was to follow the road for several hundred feet. My plan was to keep Henry to my inside, his head up and level with my knee—with James's help.

"You know Tiff's not very good on the road," Bean told us doubtfully.

No surprises there.

"We've only got about half a mile before we get to the yard," James assured her. "Tuck her on the inside of Moth behind Drummer and Henry. She'll be between Moth and the bushes, and the others will give her confidence."

But as soon as we turned onto the pavement, Henry dropped back so that he was behind Drummer, almost pulling my arm out of its socket. Riding escort to Tiffany, it wasn't so easy for James to keep Henry going, and we couldn't ride more than two abreast. A car passed us and Tiffany did a bit of a dance—but she had nowhere to go except backward, and Bean held her tight so that wasn't an option. Henry, right behind Drummer now, went along sideways, his backside out into the road. Very helpful—not.

Then I heard a motorcycle approaching from in front of us.

"Oh, rats!" exclaimed Bean. "Tiffany dreads motor-cycles! What are the chances?"

"Is that one of those two-wheeled dragon things that make a terrible noise?" I heard Tiffany say, her voice rising.

"Nothing to worry about, Tiff, get a grip," I heard Drummer try to reassure her. Good old Drummer, noth-ing causes him to lose his cool. I would have patted his neck in gratitude—if I'd had a hand free, which I didn't.

"Do you think you could work with us a little here, Henry?" Drummer asked as I leaned farther backward to keep hold of the stirrup leather.

"Why should I?" I heard Mrs. Bradley's Dales reply sulkily. "You guys are pathetic the way you always do as you're told."

The motorcycle came into view and, mercifully, the rider slowed right down when he saw the ponies. I could see his passenger rider behind him, tapping him on the shoulder and waving his arms around as though he was urging him on.

"Don't be stupid!" I muttered under my breath, aware that Tiffany was starting to jog and bounce around behind us, causing Moth to step farther into the road. Then there was silence as the motorcycle rider shut off his engine completely.

"Thank goodness!" I heard Bean sigh, and she talked encouragingly to Tiffany, who was muttering to herself and shaking poor Moth around like a pinball machine. But I couldn't worry about Bean. I had my own problems— Henry, taking advantage of the situation, pulled back farther and farther, dragging me back with him. To keep hold of the stirrup leather I had to lean right back over Drummer's quarters.

"What are you doing up there?" Drummer asked me. "This is hardly the time to lie down."

"Tell me something I don't know!" I muttered under my breath. "James!" I yelled. "You're slacking back there!"

"Sorry, got my hands full here!" James shouted back, unable to help me.

"You guys are spineless," I heard Henry continue, between orchestrating the whole situation. "You're basically puppets."

The motorcycle passenger rider was getting off the bike. My arm felt like it was being pulled out of its socket as Henry made a medieval torture rack seem like a fairground ride.

"We are *not* puppets, *actually*!" I heard Tiffany say indignantly. "If you paid attention, you would know that we're even now planning a reb—"

"Shut *up*, Tiffany!" I heard Drummer shout. "*Someone* can hear you!"

Henry stopped altogether. I considered letting go but decided I really couldn't let Mrs. Bradley's pride and joy loose on the road (however tempting that was), so I gave a desperate tug instead. Sensing victory, ever-helpful Henry jerked back and I went with him. For once, my brain actually kicked in and, blessing the newfound confidence I had discovered doing backward roll dismounts and hanging on to one side of Drummer over jumps, I hastily quit my stirrups, dropped my reins, and threw my right leg over Drummer's neck, grabbing the reins again as I slipped off over his left-hand side to land on the pavement on my feet, reins in one hand, the stirrup leather attached to Henry in the other.

"Where are you going?" I heard Drummer ask me,

looking around in bewilderment as I yanked testily on Henry's head collar.

Out of the corner of my eye, I saw the passenger rider walking toward me, unfastening his helmet, and lifting it upward. My heart sank. I'd known car drivers to hurl abuse at horse riders, telling them to get off the road—like they own it. They didn't seem to understand that sometimes it's the only way to get from one bridle path to another, and we were only on it today because of Henry's impromptu adventure on the baseball field. I hoped there wasn't going to be shouting. I took a deep breath, intending to thank the bike rider for switching off his engine before his enraged passenger rider could get a word in edgewise.

But as the passenger rider came menacingly toward me and as his head was finally released from the helmet, a cascade of blond curls tumbled down. My mouth fell open in amazement—and stayed there.

The passenger rider, dressed head to toe in black leather, was my mom.

CHAPTER 6

"PIA, ARE YOU ALL right? Did we make you fall off?"
Mom asked anxiously, staring at my face for signs,
presumably, of pain.

"No, no, I'm fine," I assured her. "Look, I landed on
my feet." I wasn't fine. I was a mess—what was my mom
doing on the back of a motorcycle. *Motor*cycle! I had so got
the wrong end of the stick, as usual. And leather, whatever
next? I mean, I'd been right about the package—what had
been in it was almost kinky.

"Hello, Mrs. Edwards," chanted Bean and James behind
me. I was sure I could detect an undercurrent of smirking.
No wonder—my mom was a *biker chick*. I'd never live it
down. Henry, oblivious to my murderous mood, stuck his
head down to eat the grass on the shoulder of the road. I
hauled it up again. He was starting to get on my nerves.
Correction: I had one nerve left, and he was *on it*!

"I asked Mike to stop when I saw the horses and then,
when I saw it was you—hello, Drummer—I couldn't believe it. And then when I saw you fall off…" my mom began.

"I didn't fall off!" I insisted. "I was pulled off! There's
a difference!"

A car pulled up behind us all, and Moth's anxiety level rose.

"Look, we'd better go," said James.

"Yes, yes—we'll follow you," said Mom.

"No, Mom, we'll be fine—the gate to Laurel Farm is only around the corner. Just let this car past, and we'll be there in two shakes. Go on with your…your ride."

But she didn't. She waited until we'd turned into the drive, and then I heard the motorcycle slowly following us. I couldn't believe it—my mom in leather, *at the yard*. I could imagine Cat's reaction. Would my mom ever tire of finding ways to embarrass me?

Cat wasn't at the yard, thank goodness. I shoved Henry into his stable, glad to see the back of his black tail and wishing we'd left him at the baseball field for someone else—or not—to find, then I put Drummer away.

"Your mom's still experimenting, I see," he said as I took off his bridle.

"I'm not in the mood," I told him sharply.

"Still trying to find herself, is she?"

"Leave it!"

"She's entitled to her hobbies, isn't she? Just like you are?"

"Don't side with her. You're *my* pony, remember?"

"Oh, and there I was thinking you were *my* human."

"Always have an answer for everything, don't you?!"

"You noticed!"

The motorcycle was parked on the gravel. It was big and red, and it had writing all over it. The rider was beside it. He wore red leather and a black and red helmet, which he was unfastening. I held my breath. What was it going to reveal? A hairy biker? Bearded with flowing locks tied back in a ponytail? Earrings? Tattoos? What had my mom attracted now?

The helmet gave way to an ordinary looking male face, about the same age as my mom. Short, brown hair, blue eyes, no visible holes in ears—or anywhere else. He nodded to me and arranged his features into a smile. Weren't all bikers shady-looking with skull-and-crossbones jewelry? Didn't they have lots of chrome on their bikes and leather tassels and bandanas with skulls? And tattoos? No chrome—except the exhaust pipe. No tassels. No bandana. No skulls. The tattoos could still materialize, once the leather was off, I guessed. Better not go there. I was surprised by how normal my mom's new boyfriend seemed. I'd been a victim of my own prejudice. Again.

"Are you sure you're all right?" Mom asked me again.

"Absolutely!" I said. "But let's talk about you. You're a surprise—a biker chick!"

Mom blushed. "I didn't know how to tell you. I've been riding passenger on the bike for a couple of weeks now, and you have to have the right gear. Um, I was going to mention it, but I didn't think you'd approve. I did tell you Mike rode a bike."

"Er, well, like I said, it's a surprise," I mumbled, guilty as charged. I thought of what Drummer had said about Mom being entitled to her hobbies. I thought of it because he was nudging Mom for the treats she always brings him.

"Sorry, Drummer, I didn't know I'd be seeing you,"

Mom apologized to him, stroking his forelock. "Pia, find something for Drummer. He's starving!"

"He's not starving, he's too fat, but I've got some carrots in the barn," I said. "I'll get them. You stay here."

"You were keeping those quiet!" remarked Drum. "And who are you calling fat? And for your information, I am starving!"

I galloped to the barn—James and Bean were there with Katy, and when they saw me, eyebrows were raised.

"What?" I said, the shock of seeing my mom making me defensive. I was not in the mood for them to be sarcastic.

"Your mom's awesome!" said Katy.

"What?" I said again, only differently this time.

"Yeah—good for her, riding a bike," agreed James. "It's a beauty too, a Ducati. I'd love one of those when I'm older. It's a great bike!"

"I know you're saying something because your mouth is moving," I told him, annoyed that James was gaga about the bike, "but all I'm hearing is blah, blah, blah!"

"The leather gear is really cool," said Bean. "I'd love to ride passenger. Do you think your mom's boyfriend would take me for a spin?"

"You are kidding, aren't you?" I asked her. "You are riling me up, right?"

"No, I'd love to go for a ride. I bet it's great!"

"Yeah. I wish my old man was a biker instead of being into those model airplanes he flies every Sunday," complained James. "Boooring!"

I grabbed the carrots and ran. Either they were crazy, or—and this wasn't altogether impossible—I was. I gave it some thought as I ran back to Drummer's stable. Mike was stroking Drummer. Drummer was being the perfect pony, like he always is when Mom's around.

"Hi!" said Mike, grinning and giving me a wave.

He looked normal. He even sounded normal, but he couldn't be normal because he was seeing my mom, and none of mom's boyfriends have ever been normal. Fact. But I smiled at him anyway, and I felt Mom relax a bit. So I smiled some more because I really wanted her to enjoy herself and not be uptight because of me.

"Nice pony," said Mike, peering over Drummer's half door and giving him the once-over. "Part Arab, right?"

"Er, yes," I said, almost falling over. Had my mom told him?

"My sister had a pony when she was younger," he explained. "A gray Arab called Mabel. I rode her a couple of times—she was great. Very fast."

"Mabel doesn't sound like a name you'd give an Arab," I said doubtfully. This day was turning into surreal central.

"Oh well, Mabel wasn't her real name—but no one could pronounce that, so Bernie just called her Mabel."

Bernie didn't sound like a name for a sister either. My mom questioned it too.

"Her real name's Bernice, but everyone calls her Bernie," Mike explained.

"Does she still ride?" I asked, interested.

"Yep, she lives in Australia with her husband and six children. The kids ride too."

"Six?" asked Mom, aghast.

"Yep, six. She's basically a production line."

We all stood and thought about that. Definitely not a pretty picture.

"Well, babe, shall we be on our way?" asked Mike, looking lovingly at the Ducati. I wondered whether he looked at my mom that way. Decided I wouldn't mind too much if he did.

"OK, Mike—Pia, I'll see you later. You are not to ride on the roads again. You always promised me you wouldn't. Do you hear me?"

"Yes, yes, I told you it was an emergency. We never go on the road usually—no need with all the bridle paths around here," I assured her. "Besides, Mom, if you're allowed on the road on the back of a motorcycle, I don't see how you've got a leg to stand on. Motorcycles are so much more dangerous than ponies."

"Well, I'm a grown-up," Mom said, going slightly pink, "and don't push it."

Then I watched as she crammed her head back into the silver helmet, clambered somewhat ungracefully aboard the back of Mike's Ducati, and disappeared down the drive in a cloud of dust, perched precariously on the back of the red and silver machine. It didn't look very comfortable. I mean, there were only two wheels and a tiny little seat—not like cuddly Drummer with a leg at each corner and a nice long neck in front of you (when it wasn't down between his front legs due to him bucking).

"What next?" I said to myself.

Drummer kicked his door. "Got any more carrots?" he asked me.

"Did you see that?" I asked him, not quite believing what I'd seen.

"It's all horsepower," said Drum nonchalantly, waggling his ears as he gazed after the bike.

I supposed it was.

CHAPTER 7

"HEY, PIA, WHAT DO you think you're doing?" Catriona yelled at me, her face screwed up in fury. And for once, I didn't blame her for being so rude. Sophie had arranged for jumps to be formed into a diamond shape to allow us to jump in and out of a box diagonally across the school, and half of us were jumping from left to right, the other half right to left, crossing in front and behind one another as we jumped. Drummer had suddenly sped up as we landed over the first jump, almost jumping on top of poor Bambi, causing her to swerve. To make matters worse, the jumps were no longer the poles but white broom handles, clutched at each end by our four helpers. Sophie had roped in Nicky, owner of the ancient pony Pippin and Bethany's mom, to join Mrs. Bradley and Leanne. The trouble was, broom handles were much shorter than jump poles and required not inconsiderable courage on the part of the helpers doing the holding. It also meant we had to steer as though our lives (or, more correctly, someone else's) depended on it. When Mrs. Bradley had asked in a trembling voice whether it wouldn't be better to use the jump poles, or even just the jumps, Sophie had waved her hand in the air as if to push away the idea.

"Oh no, the broom handles are light and easy to hold—and of course, they make much more of a spectacle for the audience. There's much more an element of danger," she'd assured her.

"Yes, dear, that's what I mean," Mrs. Bradley had said. But Sophie had decided, so that had been that. Even grown-ups didn't argue with Sophie.

James had been all for it.

"Wow, what a great idea!" he'd said enthusiastically.

"It does sound perfect!" agreed Katy.

"I'm glad all the people with ponies who are excellent jumpers and don't freak out agree," Bean had grumbled, looking doubtfully at the short broom handles.

"Tiff will get used to it," Katy had soothed her. And Tiffany had. She'd hardly looked at the handles, which was a surprise. "She's more likely to freak out at Declan's clothes," Katy had whispered.

Our fourth helper, Declan, did have a very unique style. He was as tall as James, although not as skinny, and his hair was black and blond. He was, I had to admit, sort of cute. He'd only been to two practices, but both times he'd worn baggy, checkered pants and a huge sweatshirt riddled with holes. He and Cat shared the same, neat features, only Declan's hair was longer than his sister's. He didn't scowl so much either.

Cat was scowling now, furious that I'd collided with her.

"Sorry!" I yelled into the air, unable to address my apologies directly to Cat—that would be too much—but unable to defend myself and inwardly murdering Drummer. What was he playing at? I poked one side of his withers, just to let him know I wasn't happy, but he stayed silent, which wasn't like him.

The trouble was we weren't the only ones messing up. Just as we all thought we were getting the hang of the activity ride, everything had started to go wrong—the ponies seemed to lose all sense of direction. When Cat and Bambi turned right and Drummer and I were supposed to go left, Drummer, infatuated with Bambi, suddenly ignored all my aids and followed her brown and white backside like his nose was glued to her tail. Wrong! Just as I had been congratulating myself on remembering where I had to go, and at what speed, it was now going very, very badly.

Sophie was not sympathetic. "Get it figured out, Pia!" she instructed me as Drummer shadowed Bambi for the third time in our practice after school. "If you can't get it right as a leader, your ride has no one to follow."

"Sorry!" I said, grimacing. Then I had a word with Drummer. "What are you doing?" I asked him.

"What?" he asked, all wide-eyed. "Am I doing it wrong?"

"You know you are!"

And then Tiffany, who we thought had gotten the hang of jumping the row of five jumps, suffered a relapse and kept running out.

"Sorry, my fault!" Bean yelled, cantering around for another, abortive attempt. "We'll get it right if it kills us!" she added cheerfully.

"If you don't," threatened Cat, "we might kill you!"

"Steady now, Cat!" Sophie scolded her.

"Bean's trying her best," said Dec, earning himself a scowl from his sister. "And besides," he added, scowling back, "you and Bam-Bam aren't exactly perfect—she and that brown pony act like they're glued together!"

"Shut up, Declan, you know I hate when you call Bambi that!" screamed Cat. "And you can't talk, you're acting like a love-struck wimp yourself!"

Drummer wasn't the only one in love. It was obvious to everyone that Declan was absolutely head over heels for one of the activity riders. Obvious to everyone, that was, except the object of his desire—Bean. His eyes followed her around the school like a lovesick puppy. Katy thought it was cute. Cat thought it was sickening. James thought it was hilarious. No one was telling Bean. "Let her work it out for herself," James had grinned. Of course, with Bean, that could take some time.

Even Dolly managed to mess up using the broom handles, knocking them out of Mrs. Bradley's hand every time with an exaggerated, "Whoops, clumsy me!" When Bambi put in a couple of refusals, which caused a massive pileup, Sophie waved her arms in the air and brought everyone to a halt. "What is up with you all this evening?" she asked, shaking her head.

We hung our heads in shame.

"You'd think the ponies would get better, knowing what was expected," said Katy, twirling a lock of Bluey's black mane around her finger.

"Well, thank goodness he and Moth are up to scratch!" said James. "The rest of you are awful!"

"Thanks for that, James," Cat scowled. "Maybe you should try being leading file—it's easy when you've got someone to follow."

"Don't think I couldn't!" James replied cockily. "I'd rather be leading than stuck back here behind Pia who doesn't seem to know her right from her left."

"Excuse me for not being perfect!" I replied, hurt, annoyed, and a bit guilty. I did sometimes get my right and left mixed up. It was only one of the worries I had about being a leader in the activity ride. I couldn't always remember what I should be doing and where I ought to be doing it. It was nerve-racking.

Somebody snickered. I looked around but couldn't see anyone who wasn't looking either thunderous or miserable, so I decided I must have imagined it.

"Maybe you all need a nice break," suggested Mrs. Bradley, eager to keep everyone friendly. She had taken it upon herself to be Mrs. Positive.

"Or a talking-to!" growled James, who had adopted the role of Mr. Negative.

"Give it up, James. We're all trying our best!" Katy told him angrily.

"OK, that's enough arguments. We can't keep having breaks. We don't have time for that. Let's do it once more," said Sophie. "We'll try the broom handles again. Everyone get into position."

"Try to get it right. I keep seeing my life flashing before my eyes," Leanne begged us, wearily picking up the handles with a dramatic sigh. I think she took theater a bit too seriously at school and was clearly born for soap operas. When she wasn't looking bored, she was flicking back her hair or examining her nails.

Off we went, and we were doing quite well—if you didn't count Tiffany going too fast and Bambi hesitating at every jump—when Moth suddenly veered to the side and missed out a broom handle altogether, pushing James over to the school gate and standing there all wide-eyed as though she couldn't quite believe what she'd done. It was totally out of character for James's chestnut mare.

"Now who needs a talking-to!" yelled Katy, glaring at James. "You're just as bad as everyone else!"

James went scarlet. "OK, so I got it wrong," he mumbled. "I don't know what got into Moth. She's never done that before."

There it was again—that snicker. Who was doing it? I looked around again, but everyone was deadly serious, annoyed at how badly things were going. Who could possibly think it was funny?

"Who is that snickering?" I asked.

Everyone looked blank.

"It's not exactly a laughing matter," said Cat, scowling at me.

"I know that—but I heard someone giggling," I insisted. "Who was it?"

"I didn't hear anything," said James, and everyone else murmured in agreement.

Things didn't get any better: Cat was suddenly unable to keep Bambi at a steady pace, which meant that one minute we were all squished behind her, the next, all strung out like laundry on a line. Moth missed another two broom handles, Drummer jumped one broom handle then stopped altogether, putting his head down to scratch his knee with his teeth so that I practically dive-bombed over his head, and Dolly landed badly and actually dropped to her knees, giving Sophie cause to clutch her heart in dismay as she ran over to check that she was all right. She was.

We were, as James had said, awful.

"Right, that's enough for tonight," said Sophie, shaking her head again. She was doing a lot of that lately. "We'll try again tomorrow—just for a short ten-minute session to run through the whole ride. Let's hope we can all do better than tonight. Thanks, everyone! Oh, there's my phone. Hello. Hello."

Everyone was despondent, and we hung around miserably after Sophie, Mrs. Bradley, Leanne, and Nicky disappeared back to the yard.

"I don't know what's happening!" declared Cat, scowling. "We should be getting better, not worse."

"I hope Moth's not coming down with something," said James, rubbing his hands up and down Moth's mane. "She's never, ever behaved like that before."

"Oh, let's go in and think of something else," suggested

Dee. "I eat, sleep, and dream activity ride. I'm so frightened of going the wrong way or falling off when I go over onto one stirrup over the jumps."

"I know what you mean," I agreed. Something wasn't right, but I couldn't help thinking it went further than just us being bad. Something else wasn't right. Something else was out of place. What was it?

"Let's just hope we're better tomorrow," said Katy, dismounting and running up her stirrups.

"You don't have anything to worry about, Katy. Bluey was great, as he always is," remarked Bean.

Mmmm, I thought. Bluey was always good. Bluey always tried his hardest. I couldn't help thinking that was significant. What was it that was wrong? I had a lingering feeling that there was something else, something I was missing. We put the ponies away in an atmosphere of gloom. As I put on his green stable rug, Drummer stood angelically, waiting for me to fasten all the straps before he attacked his hay net.

"Are you all right?" I asked him. He never waits—food is his passion. I'm lucky to get his bridle off before he's stuffing his face.

"What? Oh yes, thank you, just fine."

I frowned and chewed the inside of my mouth. Something was amiss—and not just with Drummer. The ponies had been very quiet this evening during practice. Usually, I heard them arguing and grumbling, but I hadn't this evening. Was it that that was bothering me?

Thoughtfully, I hung up Drummer's tack in the tack room, jostling around Bean and James and avoiding Twiddles Scissor-Paws, Mrs. C.'s killer cat, asleep on the one decent chair. James was still complaining, and Cat joined in when she arrived with Bambi's tack. Bluey had been good, I remembered, and that seemed significant. Why had it? I knew it was important. I just didn't know why.

I bumped into Dec as I went out. He was hanging around under the pretense of waiting for Cat or James, but everyone knew he couldn't take his eyes off Bean. Everyone but Bean, that was.

As I road my bike along the drive toward home I thought I could hear someone snickering again. I couldn't imagine what anyone found to laugh about because it was getting too close to the date of the extravaganza for us to be struggling. We needed to be better at practice tomorrow. Frankly, we just had to be!

CHAPTER 8

WE WEREN'T BETTER. WE were worse.

"I just can't understand it…" murmured Dee as Dolly napped toward the broom handles, digging her pink-bandaged toes in and refusing to go anywhere near them.

"Bambi's started to shake her head—it's just not like her!" Cat told us. Drummer was lethargic. I could hardly get him out of a walk—and I kept thinking I could hear someone snickering and laughing again and again. It was driving me nuts!

"Well if anything, you're worse than yesterday!" Sophie remarked gloomily as we all lined up. Tiffany pawed the ground and dropped her head. Bean was sitting with one arm through her reins, the other fiddling with her plait. She'd been darting all over the place during practice, cannoning into Moth, who had jumped around as though she was being stung. Now Tiff was sniffing the school surface, snorting through her nose and pawing the ground.

"We'll try again tomorrow," sighed Sophie. "But if we're no better then, we'll have to think seriously about whether we ought to pull out of the whole extravaganza."

There were protests all around, but Sophie shrugged her

shoulders. "I'm sure you don't want to go and make fools of yourselves, do you?"

"No, we have to get better," said Cat. "We all really want to do this!"

"I know, but I'm not trying to threaten you—we can't do it if we're no good," explained Sophie. We knew she was right, but no one wanted to think about it—we all wanted to do the activity ride.

"Look out!" Sophie suddenly shouted, rushing toward Tiffany—but she was too late. Tiffany sank onto the surface of the school with a grunt.

"Ahhhh!" yelled Bean, leaping off as Tiffany rolled over onto her side and rubbed one side of her face in the sand.

"Get her *up*!" screamed Sophie, pulling the reins and shooing Tiffany before she rolled right over and broke her saddle.

I heard someone whisper, "Good one, Tiff, wish I'd thought of that!"

"Oh, Tiffany, are you all right? She must have colic!" Bean cried, dismayed.

"I don't think so. She's just trying to roll," Sophie told her. "She's not got any classic colic signs. She's pulling the wool over your eyes."

"But she's never, *ever* done that," Bean said, anxiously looking Tiffany over.

I heard another whisper: "A sit-down—great idea!"

"You could have been crushed, Bean," Dec pointed out, concerned. I saw James look skyward.

"Are you sure you're all right, Tiff?" asked Bean, stroking Tiffany's face.

"Did anyone else hear that?" I asked. I had distinctly heard a snort, like someone was trying not to laugh.

"Give it a rest, Pia, we're so not in the mood," Dee said despondently.

"OK, well if the practice has officially finished, I think I'll do some training," said Cat, nudging Bambi out onto the track to work on her lateral movements.

"Good idea," agreed James, joining her in the middle of the track. Sighing, I nudged Drummer to the outside track and worked on our trot-to-canter then our walk-to-canter transitions. Drummer perked up immediately, working on the bit and responding to my aids perfectly. It was like riding a different pony. He'd been like a plank of wood when we'd been practicing the activity ride. Now he was improving and interested in what we were doing.

"Why couldn't you be like this on the ride?" I muttered under my breath, expecting some smart-aleck reply, as usual. Except I didn't get one. Drummer stayed silent.

How often does that happen? I'll tell you—*never!* Drummer is not a pony to hold his tongue when the opportunity for back talk is presented. Oh no, not Drummer. *But he isn't above telling the others to be quiet*, I thought, my mind bumbling along of its own accord. Why, only the other day when I'd been dragging Henry—aka the magnificent black horse—along the road, Drummer told Tiffany to shut up. Someone could hear her, he'd said. So what? It didn't usually bother Drummer.

And the other ponies had been quiet to the extreme during the last couple of practices. No arguing, no sly comments, no nothing. That was odd.

Why had Drummer told Tiffany to shut up? I thought, my mind refusing to move on from that. Why did I keep thinking of that? Tiffany…Tiffany…

She had said something to Drummer. No, she had said it to Henry. What was it? Henry had accused the other ponies of being puppets…that was it, and Tiffany had been indignant, I remembered that much.

I thought furiously. It hurt, actually, which shows how little I use my brain. That was it, I heard Tiff's voice in my mind, she'd said that they weren't puppets and that they were planning something. And that's when Drummer had told her to shut up. He'd been very insistent about that.

Hmmmmm.

I thought and thought and put two and two together. The fog cleared, the clouds parted and rays of sunshine beamed down on me as everything slid smoothly into place. I'd solved it!

I was furious! Incredibly angry. But I couldn't let my feelings show, not while Drummer could hear me. Instead I took him in and very deliberately put him away, putting his blanket on him and tying his hay net. Then I kissed him good night and did all the usual things before waiting in the tack room for the others.

One by one they arrived and, one by one I asked them to stay behind for a secret meeting. I even had to ask Catriona as she was part of the team. To my surprise, instead of sneering, she agreed, looking a bit puzzled. Of course, Declan was hanging around, snatching sneaky glances at Bean, so I couldn't very well leave him out.

"What's all this about?" asked James as I pulled the tack room door shut against equine ears when everyone was finally there.

"You're not angling for another séance, are you?" asked Bean, rolling her eyes. "Not in the dark!"

"Séance? Well, cool idea," enthused Declan, nodding. Probably because it meant he'd get longer to gaze at Bean.

"Oh, great idea, Bean!" yelled Dee, getting all excited. "We can ask my grandpa for some help with the activity ride. He really made a difference last time!"

"Will you stop giving your grandpa the credit for that!" hissed Katy. "We made it happen!"

"Made what happen?" asked Cat.

"Oh, it's a long story," said James, remembering that Cat hadn't been part of it but had been on an opposing team at the time. Anything that brought up memories of the Sublime Equine Challenge at Hickstead wasn't a good thing seeing as it had caused no end of trouble between Catriona and everyone else, especially me and, ultimately, James. At least this activity ride had mended a few bridges as far as Cat and the others were concerned. A really bad idea to bring up anything that highlighted the fact that Cat and James used to go out, and now didn't. She'd fancied him for ages and was only talking to him again because of the activity ride. The best plan was to just not talk about it!

Bean took off her riding hat and ran her fingers through her hair. Declan actually gulped. Everyone noticed but Bean.

"What do you want to talk to us about, Pia?" asked Katy, getting to the point. She always did have a way of cutting through all the dross and keeping us on track.

"I think I know what's going wrong with our activity ride practices," I said.

"Don't keep it to yourself—tell us!" cried Dee-Dee.

"It's the ponies," I said dramatically. "They're sabotaging it!"

"What?" said Cat, plainly unimpressed. "Think about it, *Mia*!"

"What do you mean?" I asked, thinking she knew something I didn't.

"Really?" said Cat. "How can the ponies be sabotaging the ride?"

"Ahh, but they can. They did before. Remember?" Katy said, frowning.

It was true. Drummer, Tiffany, and Moth had withdrawn their support for our Sublime Equine Challenge attempt—only Bluey had been unwilling to let Katy down. It was the fact that Bluey had been the only pony to be incredible at all the activity ride practices that had convinced me about the other ponies' guilt. And those snickers and comments to Tiff when she had collapsed—it could only have been the ponies laughing as their plan worked so well. And the rest of the time they had been so quiet. You couldn't tell me that was normal.

"When did they do it before?" asked Cat.

"It's not important," James said breezily, determined not to revisit that particular episode. "What's important is whether Pia is right. What makes you think it's the ponies, Pia?"

I explained, and I could see by their faces that they were totally convinced by the time I'd presented all the evidence.

"Sneaky things!" exclaimed Dee. "Dolly has it coming!"

"It's no use being horrible to them," said Katy thoughtfully. "We need to be smart, and we need to think quickly. The question is, how do we get the ponies back on board for the activity ride. They have to want to do it, otherwise they'll just make things so difficult, we won't have time to get it right for the night. I mean, we all want to do this, don't we?"

"Of course!"

"Absolutely!"

"You know we do!"

"Definitely!"

"You need to ask?"

"OK then, Pia will have to persuade the ponies to settle down," James said decisively.

Oh boy, I thought. *Thanks for that. How is that going to work?*

"How's that going to work?" I asked, aware of Cat's scowl. She was obviously torn—between not wanting me to be able to hear the ponies, and the evidence before her. Plus, everyone else's conviction that I was a Pony Whisperer hindered her attempts to undermine me, and I could tell she was unwilling to go back to being everyone's enemy. I wouldn't have liked to have been in her position. Come to think of it, I didn't like being in mine much either.

"What shall I tell them?" I asked.

"Well, you could ask them why they're wrecking the ride," Katy suggested, ever the diplomat. "We haven't heard their side of the story, yet."

"Good idea, Katy!" said James. "Go on then, Pia."

"OK, I'll have a word with Drummer," I said. They all stared at me. I looked back at them.

"What?" I asked.

"No time like the present," James said.

"And no present like the time!" shrieked Dee. "My uncle always says that at Christmas whenever anyone gets a watch!"

"That's interesting," said Cat, in an ultra-bored voice.

"Sound like Christmas is a really fun time at your place," said James sarcastically.

Leaving them to argue, I walked across the yard to Drummer's stable. Looking back I could see my fellow riders' heads peering out of the tack room. So not the backup I needed.

"Er, Drummer, I'd like to ask you something," I said,

closing the stable door behind me. Drummer's body radiated warmth in the cold night, and I got close to him. The grass outside was already crisping up nicely with frost and Drummer's breath hesitated in clouds before evaporating into the still night.

"We, that is, everyone on the activity ride, is under the impression that you and the other ponies are sabotaging the ride. What do you say to that?"

"That's not a question, it's an accusation," said Drummer between chews.

"Well?"

"It could be we're not trying as hard as we should be," he agreed.

"But why? It's such a great idea, and everyone wants to do it."

"Nobody asked us."

"But it's fun!" I wailed.

"It's hard work, jumping over broom handles and poles with you all bouncing around and leaning over and waving your coats around. And it's repetitive, doing the same thing over and over again. It's totally boring. We don't want to do it."

"Oh, Drum, come on. I know the others would do it if you talked to them. Can't you just get enthusiastic about it, like we are?"

"But it's not until Christmas, and that's weeks away. No, we're all fed up with it. Do something else—on foot."

"Please. *Please*, Drummer. Everyone wants to do it."

"Everyone who's human," said Drummer. "It's not just me—everyone's fed up with it. If they want to do it, I'll go along with it. But they don't, so that's it."

"I bet Bluey isn't part of the rebellion," I said.

"Yeah, well, Bluey's taking the moral high ground. You know what he's like, won't do anything against Katy."

"He's a lovely pony!" I said. "Genuine!"

"He's a suck-up," said Drummer.

"You mean he's a shining example, and he makes you all look bad!"

"Whatever!"

"You're all total losers," I told him angrily.

"It's no good getting all mad about it," huffed Drummer.

"I am *not* getting mad about it!" I cried, totally getting mad about it.

"If you're not mad then I'm a Shetland pony!"

I wasn't getting anywhere. I took myself back to the tack room and told everyone the bad news.

"Try again tomorrow, Pia," suggested Katy. "Or have a word with Bluey. He might be able to persuade the others."

"I doubt it. Bluey doesn't seem to have much influence. Even Moth's in on it."

"Well, that's a positive thing," said James thoughtfully.

"How come?" asked Bean.

"It means she's getting more confident. When I first got her, she wouldn't do anything unless she was sure I wanted her to do it. If she's thinking for herself and making decisions, it's a good sign."

"I never thought of it that way," said Bean.

"But that's not why Bluey isn't part of the rebellion, is it?" asked Katy, looking worried.

"No, Bluey's confident to do his own thing too. He just wants to do what you want him to do," I assured her. "And it's against his principles to do anything against you."

"Well, I've gotta go. Got some really awful English homework to make up," said Bean, pulling on her gloves. "Are you coming, Pia? I'll bike to the crossroads with you. I hate it when it's dark up here. It gives me the creeps."

"I'll go with you if you like," Declan offered, his face lighting up at the thought.

"Oh thanks, Dec, but you don't have a bike, right?" said Bean. "You'd have to run all the way. You'll get tired out!"

I thought Declan would have run to the end of the earth if it meant being alone with Bean, but Bean didn't get it.

"OK, I'll be there in two seconds," I told her, putting Drummer's grooming kit in his tack box.

"I'm leaving—that's my dad's car," said Katy, dashing outside.

James disappeared to the barn to get Moth's hay net and Dee went with him. Declan wandered outside on the off chance that Bean might need help with her bicycle lights.

When I turned around, Cat and I were the only ones still in the tack room, even though she didn't look as though she was doing anything, just hanging around. *Awkward*, I thought, heading for the door.

"Um, Mia…er, Pia…" began Cat.

I stopped and turned around, ready for the usual Cat-like abuse.

"Would you ask Bambi why she doesn't want to do the activity ride too?" Cat continued. She didn't look me in the eye.

I almost fell over with shock. Was I hearing right? Did Cat just ask me to talk to her pony? Did she just acknowledge that I might, just might, be able to talk to and hear what horses and ponies were saying?

I so wanted to say something sarcastic, but this was a *big thing*. I was desperate not to be Cat's enemy anymore. I was totally fed up with it, so worn out by all the snide remarks and worrying about whether she was going to be at the yard when I was, and how things would be when she was. This was a chance I was desperate to take. So I didn't just take it, I grabbed it!

"Of course, I'll ask her now if you like," I said, nodding furiously.

"Oh no, tomorrow will do," Cat said casually. She knew Bean was waiting for me, and I was sure she didn't want anyone else to witness her comedown. Which was understandable after she'd given me such a hard time for so long.

"And only if you get a minute. Don't go out of your way or anything," Cat told me, suddenly ultra-casual. She fiddled with Bambi's saddle so she wouldn't have to look me in the eye.

"I'd be happy to do it," I assured her, smiling.

Cat almost smiled back. Not quite. She couldn't quite manage it.

Maybe that is asking too much, I thought. It wasn't as though we were friends or anything. I just hoped that this was a turning point. If we couldn't exactly be friends, we could, perhaps, not be enemies anymore.

I'd settle for that, I decided. We couldn't expect to be great at the activity ride until we'd had a few practices. It would take more than a few practices at talking to each other for Cat and I to progress beyond hostilities. I wondered just how many practices it would take. And whether we'd ever get it right.

CHAPTER 9

WHEN I GOT TO the yard the next day after school, everyone was waiting for me. Even Declan, parts of him looking out, over, and through a big woolen sweater he had on, held around him with three leather belts—although I wasn't the reason he'd turned up, obviously.

"Finally!" exclaimed Dee-Dee as I pedaled past the tack room. "Hurry up, we can't wait to hear what the other ponies have to say about their strike."

"Mmmm," I said, propping my bike up against the tack room wall and switching off the lights. "I've been thinking about how to tackle them, and it might be best if I ask them one at a time."

"Good idea!" said James. "Then they won't be able to back up one another."

"Start with Bluey," suggested Katy. "At least he's on our side."

Bluey, it turned out, wasn't on anyone's side.

"Oh, don't ask me about it, please," he said, turning around and looking at the wall when I went into his stable. Epona was safely tucked inside my riding vest, as always. I wrapped my hand around her as I confronted Bluey.

"But we know the other ponies are deliberately messing up and sabotaging the ride," I explained. "Just tell us your opinion. No pressure—we know you're not involved."

"It doesn't really make any difference whether I am or not," Bluey said miserably. "The others are so determined not to do it. They're fed up with the practices, and they're giving me grief for not siding with them."

"Is this activity ride really so bad?" I asked him.

Katy shoved her head around Bluey's door. "What's the verdict?" she whispered.

"She must know I can hear her," sighed Bluey. "Why is she asking you?"

"I don't know," I said, turning to Katy. "Go away, I don't know enough yet."

"Oh, OK," said Katy, vanishing back into the darkness.

"So are the practices so terrible?" I asked again. "We make sure you all get plenty of rest, don't we?"

"Yes, you do. They're not hard work—but the others say they're boring. They can't see the point of repeating the same work over and over again."

"But if we don't, we'll never get better," I explained. "They have to see that."

"They just say it's boring, and they don't want to do it anymore," Bluey repeated. "No point," he added. "And someone said that if we do this, who knows what other activities you'll think up for them to do. They said best to nip it in the bud right now."

"Well, we appreciate your support," I said.

"The other ponies don't," he muttered, and went back to eating his hay.

I told the others.

"We knew that already," said James shortly.

"Ask the others," Dee said impatiently.

I talked to Dolly. She told me the prospect of practices between now and Christmas were daunting and not what she was used to. Unlike Dee, Dolly loved her showbiz life and lived for lessons and the shows. I spoke to Tiffany. Same story, although she wasn't very happy with the rebellion, as she called it. She said she was just going along with the others. It was a waste of time talking to Moth as she never replied, but I slipped into Bambi's stable to get her take on it—to everyone else's amazement. I felt really excited—I hardly ever speak to Bambi due to my relationship with Catriona.

"Hi!" I began. Bambi looked up from where she'd been nosing around in her bed searching for dropped hay. "Cat asked me to talk to you," I explained.

"Don't think so," Bambi replied, dropping her nose into her straw again.

"Really, she did," I continued. "Er, it's about the activity ride."

"What about it?" asked Bambi, not bothering to look up again.

"We know you're all doing your best to wreck it so that you don't have to practice anymore."

"Yeah, well, that just about explains it," she said, rustling around. "We're putting our hooves down. You guys are being ridiculous—all that rushing around. It's got to stop. So we're stopping it. Don't try to talk us out of it. We're all of the same mind."

"Except for Bluey," I pointed out.

"Oh yeah, well, Bluey was never going to be up for it, we knew that," Bambi said.

"Tiffany's not into it either," I said.

"The majority rules," Bambi told me firmly.

I reported back, emphasizing the way all the ponies, bar Bluey and part of Tiffany, were united, so that Cat wasn't offended. She seemed to believe me—a major breakthrough, I thought. Of course, she didn't say much, what with the others there.

"Well, that hasn't been very helpful," said Dee, puffing out her cheeks and looking despondent.

"Not that it's your fault, Pia," added Katy. She and Bluey were so alike. Bean and Tiffany were quite similar too, I thought, and Cat and Bambi. The worrying possibility that I might be like Drummer slammed into my mind. I threw it out again, pronto. I couldn't face that right now.

"So what do we do?" asked James, frowning. "We can't put on an activity ride if the ponies don't cooperate."

"I still can't believe they're being so scheming," said Cat.

"I can't believe you all can't control your own ponies," said Dec, scrolling through his cell phone. "I thought you were in charge of Bam-Bam, Cat, not the other way around."

"*Don't* call her that!" screamed Cat.

83

"That's what Aunt Pam calls her," Dec replied sullenly.

"Just *shut up!*" Cat hissed.

"We can't tell your mom," Bean said to Dee. "She'll go crazy!"

Bean was right. I didn't think Sophie would be that sympathetic to the ponies going on strike.

"She's almost resigned to the ride being canceled anyway, after the awful practices we've been having," moaned Dee.

"Oh, but I really want to do it!" wailed Katy.

Everyone agreed. It was a total disappointment. We'd all been looking forward to our performance, particularly as we were getting confident at the various moves. I was particularly proud of my backward roll dismount, and I was actually remembering where to go, most of the time. It seemed it had all been for nothing.

"Well, maybe they'll have a change of heart tonight," Katy said, ever the optimist.

"Don't count on it," I replied.

We tacked up in gloomy silence. I could hear Bambi and Moth, in their stables on either side of Drummer's, being scolded by Cat and James, but I didn't think it would have any effect. I couldn't speak to Drummer, I was so disappointed with him. Knowing he was in the dog house, he didn't say much to me either. It was like it had been before Epona came into our lives. It felt weird. It felt horrible. The practice was even worse than yesterday's, and at the end Sophie shrugged her shoulders.

"This is so disappointing—I thought you were really getting the hang of the movements, but I'm going to have to put a deadline on you all. If you're no better by tomorrow's practice I will have to tell Linda we're just not up to it. Maybe we can try again next year—if she puts on another extravaganza, that is."

Nobody said anything. Nobody could explain to Sophie as it would seem as though we were tattling on the ponies—or blaming them for our bad riding. I didn't know which would be worse.

"I was so enjoying doing something different with Dolly," Dee moaned as we rode back to the yard. The ponies had all perked up and were walking with a spring in their step. They'd got what they'd wanted—victory was theirs.

I made Drummer comfortable for the night. The air was heavy with words unsaid. What could either of us say? Nothing would change things now. Silence hung in the air like a fog, and Drummer, far from acting cocky as I'd expected him to, just kept quiet. I bolted his door and hung his tack on his pegs next to Tiffany's tack. One by one the others drifted in and put their tack away. The mood was one of gloom, gloom, and more gloom.

"Oh well," sighed Katy. I waited for her to continue, but she didn't.

James appeared, and he was in a really bad mood. He threw Moth's saddle on its peg. He was mad enough to grasp a corner of the top rug on a pile Twiddles snoozed

85

on and tweak it abruptly with a jerk, causing the tabby to awaken with a start, his green eyes wide with fury as he tumbled to the concrete floor, landing on his feet—of course.

"James!" shouted Katy, dodging quickly out of the furious cat's way. "What are you doing? He'll just go for the person he's closest to!"

"He's got too much power, that cat!" James said, but I noticed that he stepped to one side as Twiddles, mustering as much dignity as he could, sauntered out past him into the yard and headed off for the barn where bales of hay beckoned for him to sit on undisturbed.

"Don't let Mrs. C. see you mistreating her favorite feline," warned Dee. "You'll be in so much trouble."

"I can't believe Bambi would do this to me," murmured Cat. I hoped she wasn't going to start on again about me *not* being a Pony Whisperer, just because she didn't want to face up to her pony being mutinous. This crisis seemed at least to have put her feud with me on hold. Could the truce possibly be permanent? I hoped so.

"There has to be a way to win the ponies back," said Bean, heaving herself up onto the rug pile vacated by Twiddles. "There just has to be. Oh, this is nice," she added, patting the rug. "It's still warm."

"Well, come up with it, then!" said James, still fuming.

"You'll get cat hairs on your butt," Dee told Bean.

"She's only trying to help," Declan said, defending Bean and glaring at James. James didn't bother to reply.

"Getting moody won't solve anything," I said.

"Pia's right," Katy agreed. "And so is Bean. There has to be a way to get the ponies wanting to do this activity ride. And I vote we all put our thinking caps on, instead of being mean to Twiddles and getting all angry with one another, and come up with some ideas."

"Katy's got a good point," said Cat. "It's better to do something rather than just give up and moan all the time."

"OK then, we'll meet here tomorrow evening an hour before practice and share ideas," Katy said firmly, meeting everyone's eyes so no one thought she didn't include them. "And everyone has to have at least one idea to get the ponies on our side. Agreed?"

"One idea each?" asked Dee, looking doubtful.

"Yes," said Katy. "And séances don't count," she added as Dee opened her mouth. Dee closed it again, having been headed off at the pass.

"No exceptions. OK?" Katy said, looking at us all.

Everyone agreed, including James. Even Declan nodded—between snatching glances at Bean.

"But if we can't think of anything," James said, unwilling to let Katy have the last word, "and the ponies still refuse to do the activity ride, we're pretty powerless."

He was right, of course. If we didn't get our act together in time for tomorrow's practice, Sophie would call the whole thing off. Without a breathtaking, fabulous, mega, totally workable, pony-friendly, world-ending plan to end all plans, the ponies would stay on strike.

And there wasn't a thing we could do about it.

CHAPTER 10

"OK, LET'S HEAR YOUR ideas," ordered Katy as we all huddled together in her part of the barn. It was totally different to Bean's corner—Katy's hay was stacked neatly, Bluey's purple turnout rug hung on a rack her dad had made her for it, and neat plastic trash cans held Bluey's feed safe from rats. His purple head collar swung neatly from a peg, the rope wound correctly, next to three filled hay nets. Bean and I sat on a bale of hay, Dee and Cat were sitting on upturned buckets and James had hoisted himself onto one of the plastic trash cans. Declan positioned himself next to James because from there he had the best view of Bean. Katy stood in the middle. She had taken charge of the situation and wasn't relinquishing it to anyone.

"Who's first?" Katy looked around at us.

"I vote we get tough," said Cat firmly. "We can't have the ponies dictating to us like this. We'll just have to force them to do it."

"How?" asked James.

Silence. No one liked the idea of being horrible to their pony. I knew Cat wouldn't get tough with Bambi either, for all her fighting talk.

"We can't force them not to knock the jumps down, or run out, or do any of the things they've been doing to sabotage the ride," Katy pointed out. "It just won't work. What's your idea, Dee?"

"Oh don't ask me. I've been awake all night thinking and thinking and thinking. I almost fell asleep in math class today and again in media studies. The only reason I'm not in detention is because I said I didn't feel well."

"So you don't have an idea?" asked James, with an edge to his voice.

"Only that we could do a séance…"

There were cries all around as everyone despaired.

"It worked last time!" Dee insisted.

"What last time?" asked Cat angrily. No one told her.

"How about you, James," said Katy, eager to move things on and away from séance talk. "Tell us your idea."

"Well, I got to thinking about how Moth had been treated before I got her," James began, "and I wondered whether we could work on the equine guilt-trip thing."

"Explain," demanded Katy.

"Oh, you know, tell the ponies how good they've got it with us, not having to work all day, or pull carts in Cairo without being given a drink, or lugging bricks around the brick kilns in India, you know how some poor equines have it so tough in other countries. Our ponies just eat, sleep, go out in the field, and all we ask in return is for some cooperation in the form of this activity ride. It isn't exactly much to ask, is it?"

"That might work," said Cat, nodding.

"I don't know," I said doubtfully. Drummer was always going on about how much work I gave him—although I didn't think an average of an hour a day was exactly taxing, he seemed to think it was.

"Well, what's your idea, then?" said Cat huffily—like I'd rained on her parade when actually it had been James's idea.

"I could only think that Drummer is so motivated by food, it might work to put a hold on treats until the ponies help us out," I said. It sounded lame, I knew. It didn't sound particularly nice either, but I was really upset with Drum.

"We'll add that to the list," said Katy, not over enthusiastic about it. "Bean?"

"Yes?" answered Bean, looking up.

We waited. Nothing happened.

"Your idea?" continued Katy, raising her eyebrows.

"My what? Oh, oh my idea! Oh yes. Well, I just thought, I mean, it isn't a very good idea, and I haven't really thought it through or anything, but it might just work, I mean if no one else has anything better, or if we've tried everything else, it could just, possibly, if we timed it right and thought about how to put it. I mean, it could work. Maybe."

"What could?" I asked.

"My idea," said Bean.

"What. Is. It?" asked James very slowly.

Bean gave a start. "Oh, well I just thought, I mean, I wondered…"

"Just say it, Bean, for goodness', sake!" yelled Cat. "We're all considerably older now than we were before you started, and we still don't know what your idea is. So *tell us!*"

"OK, OK, hold your horses! Jeez!" moaned Bean. "My idea…" Everyone leaned forward, and I heard James hiss that it had better be good. "Is that we appeal to the ponies' better nature."

"I'm not sure Drummer has a better nature," I mumbled.

"What do you mean?" asked Dee.

"Er, well, you know. Um, I'm not quite sure, but it could work."

"But how, exactly?" asked James.

"Just appeal to their better nature," said Bean. "You know, say it's for a good cause and all that."

"They know that," said Cat.

"Well, it might work," said Katy brightly.

"Let's hear your idea, Katy," said Dee, still miffed about the séance being such a nonstarter.

Katy's idea was put on hold as there was an almighty crack as the trash can lid James was sitting on caved inward under his weight.

"Ouch!" said James, his backside wedged into the trash can, his legs hanging over the side.

Everyone collapsed laughing.

"Yeah, yeah, very funny," said James. "Pull me out

Dec, will you?" Declan took his arm and yanked until James was upright again and brushing coarse mix off his riding pants.

"You fatty, James, you've broken Bluey's feed bin!" moaned Katy, inspecting the damage. The lid had broken completely in half.

"That'll be all right," said James. "Some duct tape will fix it."

"Where were we before James's weapon of mass destruction went to work?" asked Dee-Dee.

"My idea," said Katy, looking miffed at James. "I just thought we could ask the ponies what would motivate them to do this activity ride. We haven't thought of asking them what they would like in return. It could be something simple like a week off after it all or a special treat. I thought it would be worth trying, anyway."

"That's the best idea!" said Cat.

"Yes, good one, Katy," said Bean.

"Might work," agreed James.

"And if it doesn't, we could still try the others, one by one," said Dee hopefully.

"Give it up, Dee," sighed James. "The séance is just so not going to happen."

I hoped not. It was one thing crouching over a Ouija board in broad daylight in the middle of summer, but quite another when it was dark and I had to ride my bike home alone.

"OK, we've got a half hour before our practice is going

to start," said James, looking at his watch. "I vote we meet the ponies in the school in ten minutes and give Katy's idea a whirl. If it's a no-go, we'll have time to try the other contenders out before Sophie and the others arrive."

"Yeah," agreed Katy, "it's make-or-break time. Let's go!"

CHAPTER 11

WE ALL STOOD IN a circle in the school, the ponies' heads pointing toward the middle, like the spokes in a wheel.

"Go ahead, Pia," said Katy. "You put it to the ponies. Ask them what they want in return for doing the ride."

I asked them. I explained about how we wanted them to be on board with the whole ride idea. How we didn't expect them to do all the work for nothing and how we would be happy for them to have a week off after the ride or whatever they wanted. They only had to name it, I said.

After a moment or two, Bambi replied.

"No, thanks. We thought you might come up with an incentive scheme, but we, all of us, feel that if we give in this time, who knows where it will end. So sorry, the answer is no. Thanks." I told the others.

"Try James's scheme—I mean, idea," whispered Katy.

So I did. Told the ponies how, if they lived in some countries abroad, they'd have to work all day, without enough food or water, be beaten and overworked. Wouldn't they do this activity ride for us and be grateful that their lives were so much better than those poor abused animals?

Apparently not. The answer was still no. They sympathized, they said, but no. Sorry.

"Try Bean's idea," Katy hissed. Everyone nodded.

"What was Bean's idea?" I hissed back.

"Er, oh yes, appealing to their better nature," explained Katy.

"Don't you think we're barking up the wrong tree with that one?" I asked everyone. "Bearing in mind that the ponies didn't buy the abused equines abroad tactic?"

"Try it anyway," said James.

So I did. Told them we thought they were wonderful to have been so good during the first few practices and were sure they could do the same for the remaining ones. Said that we were all dying to do the extravaganza, and that all the ponies would be stars on the night and greatly admired by all, not to mention being thoroughly thanked by us. Same story. No. I didn't even get a sorry out of them this time. Better nature? Some chance!

"That's it, then," sighed Katy. "That's all the best ones used up."

"We could…" began Dee.

"Don't go there, Dee!" threatened James.

"Won't the ponies even consider any of our suggestions?" Katy asked, unable to quite believe it. Her bewilderment was understandable—Bluey was such a genuine pony and not on the others' side at all. She couldn't understand how they could feel so strongly about it.

"They just refuse to consider anything I've put to them," I explained. "It's like pushing a boulder up a hill."

"But they're being so, so unreasonable!" Katy said, her voice rising.

"Yes, I know, I keep telling you!" I said, my voice doing the same.

Katy went into one. "Honestly," she ranted at the ponies, "I'm so disappointed in you all. I'd have thought you'd all want to help a worthy cause like Riding for the Disabled, but instead you're all behaving in a petty manner and rebelling and being so mean you could all take joint first prize in a Who's-the-meanest-pony-ever? competition. Except for Bluey, of course." She threw her arms around her blue roan pony's neck. "I love you, Bluey!" she gulped. Bluey nuzzled her shoulder. There was a silence. A really thick, heavy silence that hung on the air like fog.

Then Drummer spoke. "What did you say?" he asked, very deliberately. Katy, still buried in Bluey's neck, couldn't hear him, so I repeated extracts for him.

"She said you'd all take joint first prize in a…"

"Not that part!" said Drummer, shaking his head, his bit jangling.

"And that you're all being petty and rebelling…"

"No, no, before that," snorted Drummer impatiently. I was aware of the other ponies leaning toward me as though whatever I said next was going to be the most important thing to be said in the world. *Ever.* Gulping, I thought back.

"That, um, you would want to help a worthy cause like

Riding for the Disabled?" I mumbled, aware suddenly of the significance.

The ponies all looked at one another. Bluey slowly shook his head and sighed. Dolly suddenly found something on the ground so riveting, she couldn't take her eyes off it. Bambi swished her tail the same way a person would tap their fingers on a table, and Tiffany opened and closed her mouth several times. Moth, as usual, just looked all wide-eyed and worried. Drummer glared at me and screwed up his lips like he was sucking a lemon.

"Did we, er, not mention that's what the ride is for?" I whispered, my heart sinking.

My pony cast a beady eye at me in a way that made me feel I was the one who needed to be yelled at. "No," he said, "you did *not* mention that. This is the first we've heard that this whole thing is for Riding for the Disabled."

"What are they saying?" asked Katy. The others all leaned forward in much the same way the ponies had a moment or two earlier. I ignored them and turned back to Drummer.

"Didn't we?" I asked innocently. "Are you sure?"

"Yes, we're absolutely, one hundred percent sure that you did not, *not, not, not* mention this ride being in aid of the RDA," butted in Bambi. "We would have remembered."

"Oh," I said. "Well, er, does it make a difference?"

"Of course!" Bambi snapped. "What kind of ponies do you take us for?"

"You could have said," Tiffany muttered.

"Such an important fact to leave out!" said Bluey.

"Honestly!" Dolly snorted. "People!"

Moth sighed in a disapproving way.

"This is precisely why we should have been involved at the critical planning stage, right from the beginning," Drummer lectured me. "Failure to properly explain things from the start results in a breakdown in communication, leading to exactly this type of misunderstanding."

"Have you been on some kind of equine management course?" I asked him. "Or been reading a self-help book, because you're drifting into a totally different language."

"The point is," interrupted Bambi, "we should have been consulted, instead of just taken for granted—as usual. If we had been given all the facts from the beginning, this activity ride would be close to perfect by now. As it is, we now have to make up for lost time."

"Do you mean…?" I asked, my spirits soaring.

"We need to get practicing because frankly, you're all pretty useless," chimed in Tiffany.

"Come on. No time to lose," added Dolly, giving herself a shake.

"Pia," interrupted James, "if you're not too busy and you haven't anything better to do, would you mind terribly telling us *what's happening*!"

"It's back on!" I yelled back, beaming at him.

"What's back on?" asked Bean.

"Slices of bacon!" I said, trying out a joke. Nobody laughed, but then it was a pretty terrible joke.

"She's lost it!" said Cat, shaking her head—just like Bambi had done.

"No, the ride's back on. The ponies are totally up for it," I told them.

"Hold on, hold on!" cried James, holding up his hand like a crossing guard at a school crossing. "Hearing some of the conversation from your end, do we take it that the ponies didn't realize the whole ride was for the RDA?"

"That's right!" I said. "But now that they do, they're totally enthusiastic."

"Why didn't you tell them?" asked Cat.

"Me?" I asked, confused. Since when had that job been assigned to me?

"Of course you!" said Cat. "You're the one who's supposed to be able to talk to them. Why didn't you explain? All this trouble, all this holdup, could have been avoided if you'd got your act together—particularly when appealing to their better natures and all that."

"Yes, Pia, why didn't you tell them?" Dee said. I didn't need her to join in.

"They can hear all of you," I said. "You just can't hear them. Why didn't you tell them?"

"I think you could have mentioned it," murmured James. "You're the one with inside knowledge." I felt like mentioning a few choice words there and then—James is in on the whole Epona secret, so I expected a bit more loyalty from my accomplice.

"Yeah, it might have been a good idea," chipped in

Katy. "I mean, we don't know what the ponies are saying, but you might have had an idea."

How come I was taking the grief for the ponies' mutiny? How did that happen?

I was going to stand up for myself some more, but everyone started tightening their saddle bands and pulling down their stirrups so I shrugged my shoulders and did the same.

"I can't believe you didn't think it worth mentioning," Drummer murmured, shaking his head in disbelief. I felt like tightening his saddle band a notch or two tighter just to be vindictive, only he was so tubby I would probably have strained something in the attempt. With the way my luck was running, dear old karma was bound to be ready to pounce, only the way I saw it, she owed me. I didn't understand how I had come out of it so badly when I'd been the one who'd latched on to the ponies' little scheme and got them back on track. Cat had been the first to point the finger at me, I remembered. Typical! Just when I thought I was getting somewhere with her, she reverted to type.

Still, I thought, as Sophie and the others arrived, destined to be impressed by the wondrous spectacle of the activity ride suddenly hitting form, at least Cat had acknowledged that I could hear the ponies. Progress, of sorts, I guess.

CHAPTER 12

WITH EVERYONE WORKING TOGETHER at last, the ride progressed quickly. Now that we were all proficient (most of the time) in the movements and jumps, we put together the final routine to the musical track Sophie had organized.

It went like this: we all rode in, single file, lined up in the middle of the school, and gave a salute—taking the reins in our left hands, dropping our heads and our right hands before taking our reins again—and then we immediately rode off again in single file in trot. We did a few movements without jumps—splitting up and making pairs, then going across the school diagonally from the quarter markers, one at a time and narrowly missing each other (most of the time). Then we made two rides of three and rode on different reins, one going clockwise, the other counterclockwise—which was the part where I tended to get confused because I was a leader and had to remember where to go and at what speed, which freaked me out a little—and did some intricate movements with the two rides threading between and around each other. Then the jumps came in! Mrs. B., Leanne, Declan, and Nicky had to sharply manhandle the jump blocks and poles so that we had our line along the middle of the school to jump while we did one more circuit in trot—and that's when the fun started! We jumped the row simply the first time, splitting up at the top (so I was leading again) and riding down each side to meet at the bottom of the school, turning up the middle again at A to tackle the jumps single file once more. This second time we jumped with our arms outstretched, the third time we took our jackets off (putting them on once more as we rode along the side again), then we jumped over on one stirrup for the last time.

By this time, we were getting a little sweaty and the ponies were working hard. I almost had sympathy for their rebellion at about this point because I found I was puffing—and I was just a passenger. Then Mrs. B. and Co. hurried out with the jumps and reappeared with the broom handles—standing in the middle making a diamond with the handles held at hip height, at an angle so that we could jump them from the quarter markers.

For this part, we had to keep our heads on straight because this was where there was potential for pileups. We jumped in single file, one after the other, narrowly missing one another and doing our best not to take out the human wings. Then the human wings rearranged the handles into an X so that we jumped two abreast, making sure we were level with our partners. Then the human wings did another shuffle, stringing the handles across the whole width of the school, and we all jumped them in a line abreast (which was one of the trickiest parts because the line had to be perfectly straight, and the ponies needed to take off at exactly the same time for it to look good).

At the top we again split up into threes, with each ride circling back around to join the other in single file again, and we then lined up to face the audience to take our final bow. But first we had the big finish—with everyone starting their backward roll just as the one before them flipped their legs over, so that we all went down one after the other, like a row of dominoes, standing at the ponies' heads to finish.

And that, as they say, was that!

"Short, sharp, and sweet!" Sophie told us. "That's what we're aiming for. We don't want to bore the audience, just give them a crisp display and leave them wanting more. Come on, let's try it again, and James you need to slow down and use the corners. Katy, you need to cut your corners and keep up. Let's go!"

It didn't feel very crisp. It didn't feel very short or sharp either and as for sweet…well! Not only did we have to learn the routine, but we had to make sure we were level, and in the right place at the right time, going neither too fast nor too slow. Making sure the timings were spot on took concentration.

"Phew," said Katy, when we were taking a breather, "this is hard work."

"I still don't know whether I'm supposed to be in front of you, James, when we're jumping diagonally across the broom handles, or behind you," puzzled Bean.

"Behind," James told her. "Except when we're jumping in pairs, of course."

"Yeah, I know that part," said Bean.

The broom handlers were getting confused too.

"Should we be facing inward or outward?" Mrs. Bradley asked Sophie.

"Outward," Sophie said firmly. "That way, you won't scare the ponies, and you won't flinch if you see someone coming a little too close."

That didn't sound very encouraging. I was glad I wasn't assigned a broom handle to hold. Mrs. Bradley obviously agreed.

"Well, that's just it, dear," she said, in a worried voice, her gray curls bobbing as she shook her head, "it's very disconcerting hearing the ponies thundering up behind one."

"I think it's exciting," drawled Declan. "It makes it much more fun not knowing whether you're going to be still standing at the end of the routine, or pounded, face-down, into the sand, like a thumbtack!"

"I'm sure there's some law against it," muttered Leanne. "Health and safety and that sort of thing. Are you sure we'll be allowed to do it at the extravaganza? You know how hot those places are on those sort of things."

"Do you really think it's dangerous?" Nicky asked. "I have Bethany to worry about, after all."

"It's perfectly safe!" exclaimed Sophie. "Everyone is in complete control, aren't you?" She turned to us. We all nodded, only I didn't feel totally confident.

"Tell them to stop worrying," Drummer said to me. "We'll do our best to avoid them—only you riders are responsible for keeping your toes pointed to the front. We can't be responsible for anyone taken out by a stray toe."

I put Drummer's assurances to the team—missing out the toe bit. They seemed a bit reassured by it—only Dec looked disappointed. He managed to gaze longingly at Bean even as he ran around changing jumps and holding broom handles. I couldn't believe she hadn't noticed, but she seemed oblivious to her admirer—on planet Bean, as always.

The ponies were true to their word and were working enthusiastically. It made such a difference knowing they were trying as hard as we were to make the ride work. The extravaganza was only two weeks away, and we were all getting excited about it.

"What else is going on that night?" Katy asked Sophie. "Will there be anyone famous there?"

"Alex Willard is booked to give a demonstration of his natural horsemanship training methods," Sophie told her.

"He's Pia's biggest fan!" giggled Bean, causing Cat to cast me an evil look. *Thanks, Bean*, I thought.

"Can you introduce us, Pia?" asked Dee-Dee. "I so want his autograph."

"And me!" said Katy.

"You girls are pathetic to be asking for autographs," muttered James in disgust.

"Shut up, James. You don't know a thing about it!" Katy told him.

"I know Linda is planning a display with her RDA riders and ponies, of course. It should be a good night. I hope you're all drumming up lots of interest with your families and friends?"

"My mom and dad are bringing tons of people," said Katy.

"My family's coming," confirmed James.

"Our whole family's turning up," said Declan, "including Aunt Pam who's determined to see Bambi perform before..."

"Shut up, Dec!" snapped Cat. "No one wants to know our family history!" I saw her throw her brother a look that would turn most people to stone. *Talk about overreact*, I thought. Who cared about Aunt Pam?

"My dad's got a concert that night, but my mom actually said she might bring my sisters," mumbled Bean unenthusiastically.

This was news! Bean's family barely ever cared about Bean's riding. They were too busy being a famous musician (dad) and a famous sculptor (mom) and trainee famous musicians and artists (sisters) to get into Bean's chosen field.

"She might forget, though," Bean continued hopefully.

I thought of my dad and Skinny Lynny turning up. Thought of my mom, and I hoped she'd bring Mike, but not on the bike. *Mike-the-bike*, I thought. It fit. I wondered what my dad would make of mom riding passenger and wearing leather. I wouldn't put it past him to get a motorcycle—that's what men going through a midlife crisis are supposed to do, isn't it? I could picture Skinny clinging on in skintight black, her hair streaming out under her helmet like a tail. I'd have to keep them apart—it would be more than I could handle to have a whole family of bikers. Holy moly, imagine that!

"Let's try it one more time before we call it a night," Sophie said. We did, and we weren't bad, so we were all pretty excited when we took the ponies in and made them comfortable for the night.

"Wow," said Katy, carefully putting Bluey's purple saddle pad upside down on top of his saddle to keep the dust off it. "I actually believe we're going to do this activity ride after all. For a while there, I had serious doubts."

"Doubts?" echoed Dee. "Only doubts? I was certain the activity ride was doomed and destined for the scrap heap. I can't believe the ponies are so up for it now."

Cat stormed in, dumped Bambi's tack, and fled without saying anything, almost as though she couldn't bear to talk to anyone. Maybe I was imagining things, I decided.

"What's up with Cat?" asked Dee. So I hadn't imagined it. *What set her off?* I wondered. The practice had gone really well, and she and Bambi hadn't done anything wrong.

"Oh, it—oh you know, the usual," mumbled Katy, giving Dee a look.

"Oh, oh, yes, of course," Dee sighed, nodding her head.

I looked at Katy and remembered that there was still something about Cat that the others weren't telling me. Some big secret that they were all in on, and I wasn't. It had cropped up several times in the past, and no one would tell me what it was. It was so frustrating. *Would I ever be included?* I wondered. *Just what did I have to do to be a true member of the gang? Would I ever, ever find out what the big secret was?*

James arrived with Moth's tack, all upbeat after a great practice, and grinned at us all. "We're getting there!" he exclaimed. "We're going to knock 'em dead at the extravaganza, the way we're going!"

I agreed. It was going to be just perfect now the ponies were on board. Nothing could stop us now!

CHAPTER 13

THE NEXT WEEK FLEW by, and we ran through the activity ride routine another four times—just once each practice, so that the ponies didn't get bored. Our helpers were getting sharper at moving the equipment around, and Leanne was almost, almost enthusiastic.

"It's looking so cool," she told us, one evening, "and you're all getting much more accurate. I only fear for my life about three times per practice now."

"That's very funny, Leanne," laughed Bean. But Leanne stared balefully at her, without a hint of a smile.

"I'm totally serious, Bean," she told her, deadpan. "You should try holding a broom handle while Bambi jumps over it. Life affirming, that's what it is."

"I wish she'd get over herself," Bean whispered to me.

"At least she's still helping," I pointed out. "She could have quit weeks ago."

"Hummph!" snorted Bean. "She just likes being in on the action and getting into the extravaganza for free as one of the helpers. She's desperate to impress Jake Hampton, who's going to watch."

"The competition rider?" I asked. "But I thought Leanne was still seeing Stuart?"

"Yeah, she is," nodded Bean. "But Stuart's been dropped from the Pony Club team, and Leanne's interest is going down. She's ready to move on up, as they say."

"That's lousy," I remarked.

"Yup, you've got it!" Bean said.

As the day of the Equine Extravaganza grew nearer, some of us were getting sort of jittery at the practices. Others were getting cocky.

"Do we have to go over it again?" grumbled Cat one evening.

"Of course!" confirmed Sophie. "We've only got one week to go, and we can't afford any mistakes."

"Some of us aren't as good at remembering things as you are," Dee-Dee told Cat.

"Oh fine." Cat sighed, steering Bambi up in front of Drummer. Bambi and Drum started cooing over each other in a sickening, lovey-dovey way. "Let's get it over with. I need to do some more homework after this."

The practice began. Drummer felt good, swinging his back and turning in all the right places, before I needed to remind him. He was being so great, I decided I'd give him the rest of the night off once we'd run through the routine. He'd love that. *And some extra treats*, I thought.

It all happened so quickly. One minute we were jumping the jump box in the middle—we had paced it perfectly for once so that Drummer landed over our first jump just as Bambi was taking off for her second, so I was feeling a bit smug—when I heard a bit of a thud behind me, followed by an unfamiliar voice saying *ouch*, and a yell.

Uh-oh, I thought, turning around to take a look.

"Stop! Stop everyone!" shouted Sophie, and I saw her running toward Moth with a terribly worried look on her face as James threw himself out of Moth's saddle, looking toward her hind legs.

"What is it?" cried Cat.

"Oh, James, I'm so sorry," I heard Katy cry as she leaped off Bluey to stand miserably beside her roan pony, who was muttering to himself.

I still didn't understand what was wrong, but whatever it was, it seemed serious. We all crowded around Moth.

"What happened?" asked Cat.

"It wasn't Bluey's fault..." Katy began. "I was too close. I'm so terrified of getting left behind I was too close to Moth, and Bluey just caught one of her hind legs."

"Sorry, Moth, sorry, Moth, sorry, Moth," murmured Bluey, looking totally downcast. James was silent as he inspected Moth's heel, and Sophie looked grim. Poor Moth held up her near hind and looked miserable. *It must have been her unfamiliar voice I had heard say ouch*, I thought.

"Walk her around for a moment, James," suggested Sophie. "See how lame she is."

Moth hobbled around, snatching up her hind leg, reluctant to put her weight on it. "There, girl, steady now," whispered James, stroking her neck. Moth looked even more wide-eyed than usual.

"It's quite a deep cut," Sophie remarked, "and in a bad place—every time Moth moves it's going to flex and open. Are her tetanus shots up to date, James?"

James nodded dumbly.

"I doubt the vet can do anything much—it's in an awkward place to put a bandage. I've got some good stuff you can put on it, but I think it will swell up tonight," Sophie continued grimly.

"Oh, James, I'm so, so sorry," wailed Katy.

"It wasn't your fault. It was an accident," James managed to reply gallantly, even though he looked completely heartbroken.

"It's a shame it wasn't Dolly stamping on Moth," Drum whispered to me. "She's half the weight of Bluey—he's so big!"

Everyone was silent as James led a hopping Moth back to her stable.

"Practice over," declared Sophie over her shoulder as she followed James.

"Now what?" said Dee.

"Poor Moth," Bean sighed.

"Will she be all right?" Drummer asked me. I reassured him, and he told the other ponies. "Although I don't think she's going to be completely healthy for a while, looking at that cut," I added.

"How can we practice now?" asked Dee.

"We can't," Cat replied. "Moth looks set to be lame for ages, so the activity ride's not going to happen."

"Don't be so melodramatic, Cat," said Katy.

"It's true," said Sophie. "The ride relies on having an even number of riders and ponies. With Moth out of action, the ride's off. For good!"

CHAPTER 14

WE ALL SAT AROUND morosely in the tack room. It was the Saturday before the extravaganza, and the mood was one of gloom, gloom, gloom.

"It's just too cruel," complained Katy. "We've all worked so hard—including the ponies—and now the activity ride is grounded. I'm so disappointed, I could, I could…"

"What?" asked James. "Tease Twiddles?"

"Of course not, James!" Katy snorted. "Honestly, you've so got to get over that cat!"

"I can't. He's like some kind of feline dictator. He needs to be taken down a peg or two."

"What are you getting for Christmas?" I asked Dee, trying to change the subject.

"What? Oh, I've asked for the most fantastic sequined top from Urban Outfitters, but I think Mom will get me what she usually does—some new showing gear," Dee told me glumly.

"I've asked for a new cell phone," said Bean.

"So have I!" Cat said. "My one has never been the same since I dropped it into Bambi's water bucket."

"Imagine that!" remarked James.

"There must be something we can do!" moaned Katy.

"About what?" asked Bean, poking a cobweb with her whip.

"The activity ride! What do you think?" Katy yelled.

"It's not going to happen, Katy," Cat told her. "Accept that."

"Except that what?" asked Bean. Nobody bothered to put her straight.

Leanne came in for Mr. Higgins's tack. "You all look like you've been condemned to death," she told us.

"Yeah, well, you know," Dee said, shrugging her shoulders.

"It's not the end of the world," Leanne told us as she disappeared with her tack. Dee pulled a face after her.

"Will you leave that cobweb alone, Bean?" Katy asked her, annoyed. "That's the second spider you've forced to come out of that thing."

"Where?" I asked, moving away. I hate spiders. Suddenly, Mrs. Bradley appeared with a huge smile on her face. *I hope she's not going to be all happy*, I thought. I didn't think I could stand it.

"Hello, everyone!" she said, closing the door behind her and beaming at us all.

We grunted in reply, not really sharing her mood.

"I've been thinking," said Mrs. Bradley, her eyes sparkling, "and I have the perfect solution."

"To what?" asked Bean.

"The activity ride!" said Mrs. Bradley. "James must ride Henry!"

Talk about a bombshell! That got everyone's interest. We suddenly gave Mrs. B. our full attention.

"I won't take no for an answer," she continued, sticking

out her chin. *Like anyone was going to argue*, I thought. "Henry will love it, and it will be such a nice change for him. It's the perfect solution!" she repeated. "And I'd love to see him perform," she added, grinning.

"Oh, it is the perfect solution!" exclaimed Katy.

"Totally!" agreed Dee-Dee.

"That means the ride goes on. Hooray!" yelled Cat.

"That's so nice of you, Mrs. Bradley," added Katy.

James said nothing. Then he gave Mrs. Bradley one of his most devastating smiles (which I'm always hoping he'll throw in my direction, pathetic as I am) and leaped over to plant a kiss on her wrinkly cheek.

"Mrs. B., you are an angel!" he told her solemnly. Mrs. B.'s face turned bright red under her gray hair, and she looked like she might explode. If I'd known James was going to be so grateful, I'd have lent him Drummer—even though I know that wouldn't solve anything, but you know what I mean.

"Let's give it a try out right now!" said Cat. "Where's your mom, Dee?"

"I dunno, doing something in the stable, I think," muttered Dee.

Dee disappeared to drag Sophie away from cleaning the kitchen cabinets in the stable, or some other dreary task she was doing to take her mind off the nonevent that used to be the activity ride, and we all galloped off to saddle up the ponies. Meeting us at the school, Mrs. Bradley puffed up with pride at seeing James dashing on her "magnificent" black horse, also known as Henry.

"It's so strange seeing you on Henry instead of Moth," remarked Bean. I knew what she meant. Henry was built like a tank and had feathers flowing from his knees and hocks down over his hooves like skirts. I don't think Mrs. Bradley had ever pulled his mane or tail, and he had a beard and whiskers that would have done Santa proud. Unclipped, he looked like a big, black, hairy yeti next to our clipped and trimmed ponies. Henry also being about twice as wide as Moth, James looked a lot smaller on him than he did on his own chestnut mare.

"If this works, Henry is in for a substantial makeover," Katy hissed to me, steering Bluey past Drummer.

"You're not kidding," I replied. "He needs a complete overhaul."

"Now, Henry," I heard Bambi begin, "it's very simple, this ride. Just watch and learn and copy what we do. You'll catch on quickly."

Good, I thought. Henry was going to have the benefit of the other ponies' experience. He'd soon be up to speed. I hadn't bargained on Henry's attitude.

"Get lost!" he replied. "I'm not doing this stupid ride thing with you lot of roll-over-and-do-whatever-the-humans-want ponies."

"Oh, come on, Henry, do the decent thing for once," Drummer said impatiently. "You know this ride helps the RDA. We're all doing it, and it won't kill you to get on board for something worthwhile for once."

"No way," Henry replied. "I, unlike you all, have trained

my human, and she does what I want, not the other way around. I'm not part of your pathetic, so-called team. I'm not giving up my cushy life, thanks!"

Bluey shook his head sadly. "Honestly, Henry," he said, "you miss out on so much with that outlook on life."

"Pah!" replied Henry rudely. "Go preach at someone else."

My heart sank. We'd got the other ponies on board so successfully, and now we had Henry to convert. Why was nothing ever easy?

"Dear Henry is refusing to play ball," I whispered to Katy. She rolled her eyes in despair. "You're kidding!" she said. I shook my head.

"Well, James is no Mrs. B.," Katy said thoughtfully. "He might just persuade Henry otherwise."

That was true. James wouldn't be asking Henry if he minded, ever so, please, to trot like Mrs. Bradley did. James would drive Henry on with strong leg aids and keep him between his leg and hand, so Henry wouldn't have much choice in the matter. My mind flew back to the image of James urging Henry at the field fence. And Henry being his usual, unresponsive self. It didn't give me a reason to share Katy's confidence.

"OK, let's take it slowly until Henry gets the idea," Sophie suggested. "Go in your usual position, James, and we'll see how things go."

Things went badly. Despite James's experienced and firm riding, Henry found plenty of ways to ruin the ride.

He cut corners. He was inattentive at the jumps. He

went too fast when he should have slowed down. He went slowly when he should have sped up. He jumped crookedly, he stopped abruptly on landing, and he tried to pull the reins out of James's hands by thrusting his nose to the ground. All in all, he was a total pain, just like our ponies had been during their rebellion. He disrupted the entire ride, upsetting all the other ponies, who were furious.

Mrs. Bradley was mortified.

"Oh dear," she said, crestfallen. "I suppose you're just not used to my Henry, James dear. I'm sure when you get to know him, everything will be better."

I caught James's eye and shook my head. No way was it going to get better, and it wasn't James's fault.

"Can't you make Henry toe the line?" Sophie said quietly to James.

"He's a nightmare, totally unschooled and disrespectful," James explained, his shoulders sagging as he dismounted. "I really need to sort him out, but I can't be horrible to him with his doting mom, Mrs. B., sitting there watching me. The pony has no respect at all. He just ignores my instructions completely."

"Mmmm," mused Sophie, lost for words, for once. Her cell phone rang, and she turned away, lost in advice to her friend about a horse the friend was thinking of buying.

The ponies were having their own discussion.

"We have to do something. Henry's wrecking the ride," said Bambi.

"It's not fair," complained Tiffany. "I've bumped into him three times when he just stopped for no reason. It's no fun having your nose shoved into Henry's tail," she said, wrinkling her nose up in disgust.

"I think he needs a kick," suggested Drummer.

"How will that help?" asked Bluey. "We've already got Moth out of action."

"If it were summertime, and we were in the field at night, we could have a little word with our uncooperative friend and persuade him to embrace teamwork," Drummer said grimly.

"Well, it isn't, we're not, and we can't," said Tiffany.

"Hang on a minute…" said Drummer, and he turned to me. "Do you think James could make sure Henry doesn't kick anyone if we put a plan into place?" he asked me.

"I'll ask him," I said. "What sort of plan?"

"Oh, just a sort of push-Henry-in-the-right-direction plan," Drum said airily. He turned back to the other ponies. "Do you think you can lean on Henry? After all, he's your partner," he asked Tiffany.

"Are you kidding?" Tiffany replied, her ears swiveling. "He's twice my weight. He only has to lean back, and I'll cave like a cardboard cutout!"

"True, there isn't much of you," mused Drummer. "I don't understand it. You eat like there's no tomorrow."

"Worms," snapped Bambi.

"Hey!" exploded Tiffany. "It's my metabolism. I'm naturally slender! Not like you!"

"Just what are you insinuating?" demanded Bambi.

"Mares, mares," soothed Drummer, "can we stay focused, please?" Bambi and Tiffany, truce declared, paid attention as Drummer explained his plan. The ponies were to persuade (Drummer's word, not mine) Henry to cooperate by pushing him along and bouncing him into the right place. "If he stops in front of you, Dolly, you have to nip his rump. If he goes less than straight, Tiffany, it will be your job to straighten him up."

"But I've just told you, he's built like a tank, and I am *not*!" said Tiffany.

"OK," said Drum, thinking furiously, "you're more Henry's size, Bluey. We'll have to get you next to him."

"Me?" asked Bluey, not welcoming the idea. But, being Bluey, he came around. "OK, I'll take one for the team!" he declared loyally.

"Atta boy!" said Bambi.

"And if he gets too close to me," threatened Drum, "I'll give him both barrels. Is the plan clear?"

"Yes!" chorused the ponies. I half expected to see them give a high five, but being ponies, that was obviously out of the question.

"Er, Drum," I interrupted.

"What?"

"Don't you think that your plan, well, it's sort of bullying."

"Oh don't start!" exclaimed Drummer. "Of course it's bullying. You want the ride to work, don't you?"

"Well, yes, but..." I trailed off.

"We've tried to appeal to his better nature by telling him what the ride's in aid of, but stubborn Henry hasn't got a better nature. He refuses to adopt any sort of team mentality. Clearly James can't get forceful when Henry's dear mommy, the ever-so-sweet-but-totally-ineffectual Mrs. B. is in the corner, believing the sun shines from under Henry's tail, so we have to take action. If you've got any other ideas, now would be a good time to tell me about them. If not…"

I shook my head. No ideas.

"OK then!" continued Drummer firmly. "We agree that the RDA outweighs Henry's feelings, and our plan goes forward. It's not as though dear Henry is a shrinking violet and likely to be permanently damaged as a result of a few shoves here and there, is it?"

I shook my head again. It would take dynamite to damage Henry.

"Now you, Pia, have to wangle it so that Bluey and Tiff swap places. And you need to bring James up to speed so he can help. The whole plan now depends on you."

"Oh!" I said. I could do that, surely? I nodded my head this time, which made a change.

Dismounting and handing Drum's reins to Katy, I beckoned James over to the corner of the school (he left horrible Henry with Mrs. B. fussing over him) and explained about Drummer's plan. "You need to make sure Henry can't kick or bite the others," I told him. "The ponies are going to rough Henry up a bit. We can't afford any more accidents."

James looked thoughtful. "You know, I would have a huge advantage if I knew what was coming and could hear what Henry and the other ponies were saying. Will you lend me You-know-who for a while?"

You-know-who was our highly unoriginal code name for Epona. With my little stone statue, James would have a one-up on Henry. It made sense.

"Of course," I nodded, reaching into my pocket and wrapping my hand around Epona. Making sure James was between me and the rest of the team, so that no one could see the swap, I carefully handed her to James, who zipped her up into his jacket pocket.

"Thanks," he said. "That should help. Henry won't be so cocky when I can hear him and know what he's planning!"

"Now I've got to get Sophie to swap Tiffany for Bluey," I told him. "Bluey's more Henry's size so it will be an even match. You'll be riding with Katy as your partner if all goes well."

I marched over to Sophie, hoping my positive stance would help me persuade her. As it was, she didn't need persuading.

"I think you're right, Pia," Sophie nodded. "Bluey and Henry would look better together, with the two mares, Dolly and Tiffany, bringing up the rear. We'll try another run-through and hope that sorts things out. If not, I don't know what we're going to do. Honestly, this activity ride is turning into a nightmare. I've organized several of these, and this one has been the most difficult to get through.

I'm beginning to wonder whether we're just not meant to do it."

"Oh, don't say that!" I begged. "It's really fun and everyone is enjoying it. Except for Henry!"

Bean was delighted to be swapping places with Katy. "Thank goodness," she sighed, easing Tiffany along beside Dolly. "I'm fed up with James bossing me around."

"Hummph!" Katy snorted. "He won't boss me around!" She never would let James intimidate her. Bluey looked resigned, knowing he'd have more work to do in his new position.

Before I mounted Drummer, I whispered in his ear so he knew I couldn't hear him. Everything was strangely silent. It was weird not being able to hear the ponies. I'd got so used to listening to their arguments and comments that, without Epona, it was as though I had lost one of my senses. And, in a way, I had.

Knowing what the ponies had planned, I could see exactly what they were doing. Henry didn't stand a chance.

Every time the chunky black pony slowed down, Dolly bared her teeth and nipped the top of his tail. If Henry tried to kick out, James legged on like a madman, his teeth clenched in determination. Every time Henry tried to go too fast behind Drummer, I felt Drummer's back come up as he threatened to kick him. Bluey kept him straight on one side so that James only had to concentrate on riding the other side of him, and with everyone working together, Henry, somehow, got through the routine. He even stood stock-still, sandwiched between a threatening Drum and Bluey so that James could perform his backward roll off him at the end, and we all stood in line in triumph. Henry looked mutinous, the other ponies like butter wouldn't melt in their mouths.

Success!

"Phew," panted James, bent over double, his hands on his knees. "I'm exhausted."

"Oh, James!" squealed Mrs. Bradley, rushing up and patting Henry's furious face. "You were wonderful. My darling Henry is a star!"

Without Epona, I could only guess at Henry's reply—and was rather glad, for once, that I couldn't hear what he was saying.

CHAPTER 15

IT'S TIME TO SORT out what everyone will be wearing,"
Sophie declared, having called a meeting in the barn.

"Can we all dress up like cowboys?" asked Bean.

"No, Arab sheiks," shrieked Dee, bouncing up and
down on Dolly's hay bale.

"Absolutely not!" said Sophie firmly. "We want to give
the impression that we're serious riders, not circus clowns."

"Thank goodness!" said James, frowning.

"I really like costumes though," mumbled Katy.

"Does everyone have a navy or black jacket?" Sophie asked.

"Yes," chorused Dee, Bean, Cat, and Katy.

"My show jacket is gray," I said. I'd bought it with my
Sublime Equine Challenge prize money and loved it to bits.

"I only have a tweed one," said James.

"OK, let's think," said Sophie, pursing her lips. "You
don't all have to wear black or navy, but I think it would
look best if we matched in our pairs—so Cat and Pia need
to have the same color jacket, so do James and Katy, and
Dee and Bean. Both Dee and Bean have blue jackets, so
that's all figured out…"

"Leanne's got a gray jacket," said Cat. "I bet she'll lend
it to me for the extravaganza so that I match Pia."

"That's fantastic!" said Sophie. "Now we've just got to sort out Katy and James."

"No problem," sniffed Katy, grinning. "I've got a tweed jacket too. I can wear that. It's probably a bit short in the arms, but it still fits for the most part. No worries."

"Well, that was easy," sighed Sophie. "Now we all need to wear a white shirt—you've all got white dress shirts, I take it—and the same color tie. I'll get some. Cream, beige, or white riding pants—and do you want to wear short or long boots?"

"Long!" everyone yelled.

"OK, well, that was easier than I thought it would be. But I was thinking that for the ponies…"

"Won't they just wear their saddles and bridles?" interrupted Bean.

"Of course," agreed Sophie. "But I was thinking of leg bandages, just for the front legs. They always look great."

"Let's all have different colors," said Cat. She would. She always wears lots of clashing colors together. "Or even a different colored cloth on each leg!"

"That's going too far," said James. "The different color idea is OK, but let each pony have the same color on their legs. We don't want to look like clowns."

"OK," nodded Sophie, "different colors. Who wants what color? What color leg cloth do you all want?"

"Purple!" said Katy. Everyone groaned.

"We know that!" said Dee-Dee.

"I don't care," said James.

"I call green. Drummer looks cool in green," I said.

"Blue," said Bean.

"I call the yellow ones," offered Cat.

"I could wear any color," Dee told us.

"Good, I can borrow two of yours," said James.

"Let's recap," said Sophie, counting on her fingers. "Bambi in yellow, Drummer in green, Bluey in purple—of course!—and Tiffany in blue. Dolly can wear pink, and how about Henry in red? That would work really well as all the pairs will tone nicely—yellow and green, red and purple, and blue and pink. Sounds great!"

"Henry will look ridiculous in leg cloths," said James. "He has so much hair."

"Not after tomorrow, he won't," Sophie told him darkly. "I've persuaded Mrs. B. to let me clip him. He's having a hunter clip, and I'm taking off his feathers. I'm also looking forward to tackling that mane and tail with the pulling comb. You won't recognize him tomorrow evening."

"Thank goodness!" said Katy. "He was totally ruining the whole ride with his wild pony look."

"I've got an idea," said Bean.

"Let's hear it, then," Sophie said.

"If we're all having different colored leg cloths, and you're going to buy some ties, why don't we match our ties to the bandages? So I'll have a blue tie to match Tiffany's legs."

"That's a perfect idea!" cried Katy. "And I already have a purple tie!"

"No? Really?" James asked sarcastically. Katy slapped his arm.

"Mmmm, that's a good idea, Bean," said Sophie. "It will lift the whole ride."

"Won't Bean look extra blue?" asked Cat. "Blue jacket, blue bandages, blue tie?"

Sophie frowned. "Yes, you will a little, Bean. What if you wore pink, instead?"

"Yuck, pink will look awful with Tiffany's golden coat."

"How about if you have the red and James has the pink?" asked Dee-Dee.

James shook his head. "I'll tell you right now, I am absolutely not wearing pink!" he said firmly.

"OK, we've got some turquoise bandages. They would look better than blue and really lift Bean's blue jacket. And the color will suit Tiffany," said Sophie.

"That's fine," agreed Bean. "I like turquoise."

That was settled. In fact, I thought, everything was settled. Moth's substitute, the unwilling Henry, had knuckled down, accepting that he had little choice in the matter, and everyone knew what they were supposed to be doing, in what order, and when.

Every time we saddled the ponies for a practice, poor Moth gazed out of her stable longingly, neighing as we all clip-clopped our way to the school without her. She was getting better every day but was still lame. There was no way she could have done the ride—even if her cut healed by the weekend, we couldn't chance the wound opening up again. And Henry was transformed by Sophie and her clippers: from chubby, hair-smothered black hillbilly look-alike to a sleek, clean-legged, chunky riding pony. His mane and tail were neatly pulled, revealing a small white star under his forelock. The hunter clip suited him, and with his beard clipped off, and his legs clean and featherless, he looked more like a miniature warm blood than the hairy Dales pony we were used to.

"Wow!" James said, when Sophie stripped Henry's rugs off in a big reveal. "Is that my new charger?"

"Who's that and what have you done with Henry?" Katy had snickered.

Mrs. Bradley had been almost speechless when she'd seen her darling Henry.

"Oh, Sophie," she'd breathed. "He's beautiful!"

"Humph," Bean had snorted. "He's still got a long way to go to earn that title!"

"She loves him," I'd said. "It's so nice."

"I hope she'll be able to ride him OK!" Bean had replied darkly, her eyebrows disappearing into her bangs. "He'll be a bit livelier with his coat clipped off. Mrs. B. had better buy an exercise rug to keep him warm if she doesn't want to have flying lessons."

"Oh no, what if she can't ride him and we're responsible for her death-by-Henry?" I asked, suddenly worried.

"She's survived this far," Bean said, "so she must have a guardian angel looking after her."

"One thing's for sure," I laughed. "Henry's no guardian angel!"

"Maybe not," mused Bean, "but he's come to the rescue of our activity ride!"

CHAPTER 16

"A PONY WANTS TO BE tucked in his stable on a freezing night like this, with his blanket, hay net full, and deep bed under hoof," Drummer complained. "Not gallivanting about the countryside performing to people who should be sleeping in their own beds."

"It is a bit cold," I agreed, shoving my gloved hands deep into the pockets of my bright yellow down jacket. "But it's a bit early for people to be in bed," I added. "It's only five o'clock—they'd more likely be watching the TV."

"Whatever," sighed Drummer.

He'd traveled to Taversham in Sophie's luxury horse trailer, together with Dolly, Bambi, and Henry, with Dee, James, Cat, and me in Sophie's motor home. I had heard Drum and Bambi whispering sweet nothings into each other's ears throughout the entire journey, which had bored Henry and made Dolly go all gaga. Truthfully, three miles from home I'd wished I could have put Epona somewhere else so I didn't have to listen to them, but there wasn't anywhere, so I had to listen to all the cooing and lovey-dovey nonsense. It was almost as bad as listening to my dad and Skinny Lynny when they got going. In other words, totally gross!

Henry had protested in the yard about loading, but Sophie already had a cunning plan involving a bucket of feed, and Henry's greed got the better of him, allowing him to be enticed up the ramp. He'd spent the last few practices sullen and sulking, but nobody cared much. We just wanted everything to go as planned. Tiffany and Bluey had shared Katy's trailer, and we'd left in a convoy, Bean and Katy in Katy's dad's car. We could see them in the motor home's side mirrors as they followed us down the drive.

The worst thing had been leaving Moth behind. We could hear her neighing as we drove off, and we'd all felt awful for her. James stuck his fingers in his ears and screwed up his eyes—it was a hundred times worse for him, of course. It just didn't seem the same without Moth.

Now we were actually at the extravaganza I felt a little jittery. Butterflies flew around my stomach, and as soon as we parked, I wanted to go to the bathroom. There seemed to be a steady stream of cars coming through the gate and being directed to one of the frozen fields for parking. *Just how many people were coming to this display?* I wondered.

"I feel so nervous," Cat said as Sophie switched off the engine.

"Really?" I asked, amazed, thinking I was alone with my fears. "You don't look it. You always look totally composed."

"Yeah, well, I'm not. It's terrifying being leading file. I'm so scared that I'll forget where to go and what to do."

"Oh, me too," I said.

We looked at each other, suddenly shy. *Cat and I are talking*, I thought. *We're having a conversation. We're actually sharing our thoughts and fears instead of insulting each other or being rude.* Cat suddenly leaped into the back of the horse trailer and got very busy checking on Bambi, as though the thought had occurred to her too. James certainly noticed. As Cat disappeared, he gave me a look—you know, raised eyebrows. I just shrugged my shoulders at him. I suddenly realized that Cat and I hadn't been mean to each other for a long time. We'd been working so hard together on the activity ride that old grudges seemed to have faded. *Would they resurface once the ride was over?* I wondered. *Would we go back to Cat calling me the wrong name, and me avoiding her?* I so hoped not. It spoiled things at the yard, and the atmosphere had been a hundred times better since we'd been working on the ride together. It really highlighted how horrible things had been before. As we stepped down onto the concrete, Katy galloped over, waving some paper at us. "Have you seen the program?" she asked, not waiting for an answer. "The activity ride is on last. The RDA riders are performing a pantomime on the RDA ponies first of all, then there's a display by something called Jive Pony, then the intermission. Alex Willard is demonstrating some of his natural horsemanship techniques after that, and finally, it's *us*."

"Oh no," wailed Cat, "my nerves will never last until then. I was hoping we'd be on first and get it over with."

"We should be flattered," Sophie interrupted, walking over with a steaming cup of coffee from her fully equipped kitchenette. "The activity ride is the finale. We've got the best spot!"

"Woo-hoo!" said Bean sarcastically.

"Do you hear that, Drummer?" I asked him, leaping up through the groom's door and walking along the aisle to where he stood between Bambi and Henry.

"Yeah. Whoop-de-doo!" Drum said flatly.

"That's fantastic!" said Dolly, her showbiz self kicking in. "Top billing. It's like taking the championship!"

I looked at Drum, and he nibbled Bambi's neck. Bambi squealed quietly, pretending to mind. They were really sweet together. I thought back to when we'd both had to move home when my parents divorced. It hadn't only been me who had left old friends behind in our old lives; Drummer had missed his old equine friends at our last livery stable too. He had settled in almost immediately with all the other ponies at Laurel Farm, but Bambi had taken much longer to win over. I smiled. Bambi was the most important pony there to Drum. He seemed so content now that she loved him as much as he loved her, and I was pleased my wonderful pony was so happy.

"I think we'll leave the ponies in the trailer during the first half of the extravaganza," suggested Sophie, looking over Katy's shoulder at her program. "They'll be warmer in here. Then we'll get them out after the intermission and warm up while Alex Willard is doing his thing."

"Oh no," wailed Bean. "I really wanted to see Alex Willard's demo."

"Yeah, same here," complained James.

"That's such totally bad timing!" yelled Dee. "You could have had Linda sort things out better, Mom," she grumbled.

"I didn't have anything to do with it!" Sophie protested, holding up her hands and almost spilling her coffee.

"But we have to be professional about this," said Katy, sensible as ever. "We have to warm up, and that's the only time we can do it."

"Oh, I know, you're right. I just needed to complain," mumbled Bean.

"OK, are you all done?" Sophie asked.

"Let's go and look around now," suggested James. "We have until the intermission to do what we want, so why are we all standing around here?"

We went off to look around, and I kept an eye out for Alex Willard, hoping to see the great man again. The arena where the extravaganza was being held was huge, with a vast gallery with permanent seating. There was extra seating in the form of plastic chairs in the top and bottom half of the huge arena, marked off by white poles.

"They couldn't have sold that many tickets," said Katy, frowning. "There are so many seats."

"Maybe it's for the other shows they hold," I suggested. "They can't all be for tonight."

People were piling in for the extravaganza, and we lined up for hot dogs and hamburgers.

"Oh, look!" said Cat, pointing. "Trade stands. Sometimes you can get great bargains at these things, and I don't have all my Christmas presents yet." We all made our way over to stands selling horse equipment, magazines and books, and some gorgeous silver jewelry. Behind those were more stands offering handbags, horsey comforters, and cushions, and a tent with a notice declaring that you could have your fortune read by Gypsy Sylvia, fortune-teller to the stars.

"Oh wow, I've always wanted to have my fortune told," gulped Dee.

"Why does that not surprise me?" groaned James.

"I'm in!" yelled Bean, fishing in her jacket pocket for her wallet and diving into the tent.

"Ooooh, let me come with you," shrieked Dee, hot on Bean's tail.

"You're just wasting your money!" Katy yelled after them.

"Come on," said James. "Let's leave them while they do it."

"No way!" I said. "I'm staying to see what Gypsy Sylvia has to say to Bean."

"Me too!" agreed Cat.

"Definitely!" nodded Katy.

"But I thought you said...?" began James.

We all laughed. "No way are we missing this," Katy said, slowly shaking her head and grinning.

"OK," shrugged James. "I'm going to find my parents. They should be here by now."

As James disappeared, Dee emerged from Gypsy Sylvia's tent.

"What's happening?" asked Katy.

"She wouldn't let me stay and listen—she said she can only do us one at a time," Dee moaned.

"What does she look like?" I asked, imagining a woman with raven hair, hooped earrings, and a scarf around her head.

"She's blond and a little chubby. Not exactly what I was expecting," Dee explained.

Not very gypsyish, I thought, disappointed. I'd expected her to be like Jazz, the traveler girl I'd met last year.

We hung around getting cold, and then suddenly, the tent flapped open and Bean popped out. We fell on her like she'd been a missing person.

"What did she say?"

"Are you going to be famous?"

"Or rich?"

"Oh, ha, ha!" said Bean.

"Who's next?" asked Gypsy Sylvia, poking her head out. I saw what Dee meant—she should have made more of an effort in the gypsy wardrobe department—a shawl might have been more convincing than the quilted jacket and polo neck she was wearing.

"Er, I might try it in a minute," mumbled Dee, chickening out. We all fled to a quiet spot and quizzed Bean.

"Come on, spill the beans, Bean!" insisted Cat.

"She said my favorite color was green…"

"That's not telling your fortune," moaned Dee.

"And that I had a secret admirer…"

"We all know that!" exclaimed Cat.

"And he's hardly a secret. I mean, everyone knows he really likes you," said Katy.

"Gypsy Sylvia doesn't!" I said.

"Unless Bean has another secret, secret admirer, that we don't know about," suggested Cat.

My heart sank. I so hoped it wasn't James.

"What are you all talking about?" asked Bean, confused as ever.

"What else?" demanded Dee, guiding her around the subject.

"She said that my love of horses would help me through any difficulties ahead," Bean said, narrowing her eyes as she concentrated on remembering, "and that I should always remember that I was strong enough to cope with everything life throws at me."

"That's cheerful!" said Cat.

"And she said I had to always listen to my instincts because they would help me make the right decisions in my life, and that friendships I make are so strong, my friends always will understand and forgive me when I let them down."

"Not very upbeat, is she?" asked Dee. "I don't think I'll go for a visit."

"Are you OK, Bean?" Katy asked.

Bean looked worried. "I think she was trying to tell me something about the ride," Bean said.

"How did you get that from what you told us?" asked Cat.

"I'm going to mess up, aren't I?" wailed Bean, her eyes suddenly widening.

"You look like Tiffany when you do that," Cat told her.

"That's completely wrong, Bean!" said Katy. "She didn't mean that. Honestly, you shouldn't have gone in there. It's all nonsense. She can't know anything, and now you're reading tons of stuff into what she said that simply isn't there."

"What's going on—are you destined for fame and fortune, Bean?" asked James, suddenly appearing out of nowhere.

"No," cried Bean. "I'm destined to forget the routine of the ride—but you all have to forgive me. I'm so sorry in advance."

"What?" said James, bewildered.

"She didn't say that. You're not going to mess up!" insisted Katy impatiently.

"Oh look, there's Dec," said James as Cat's brother waved at us and made his way through the growing crowd of people. As always, Dec's piercing green eyes were glued to Bean's face. And, as always, Bean didn't seem to notice.

"We're going last, buddy, so plenty of time to relax," James told him as they greeted each other with a high five.

"Cool," said Dec economically.

"I'm still hungry," Bean said to no one in particular.

"I'll buy you a hot dog, if you want," offered Dec, recognizing an opportunity.

"Oh, no thanks," said Bean, wrinkling up her nose. "I'm all mixed up knowing I'm going to let everyone down."

Declan looked suitably crushed. Everyone else just groaned.

"Should have been here earlier, man," James told Dec sympathetically.

No, I thought, *James can't be Bean's secret admirer if he is sympathetic to Dec's pain.* I sighed with relief.

"You OK?" James asked me.

"Perfectly!" I said truthfully.

Katy dragged Bean off with us, leaving the boys by themselves. "Jeez, Bean, you are tactless," she said, frowning at her.

"Me? Why?"

"You could throw Declan a bone," Katy said.

"What are you talking about?" asked Bean. Cat looked skyward, and Dee groaned.

"Declan," hissed Katy.

"Declan?" asked Bean, frowning. "Why would he want a bone?"

"What Katy means, oh, clueless one," said Cat, "is that my brother really likes you, and you could be nicer to him."

"He's the secret admirer Gypsy Sylvia was talking about," I told her.

"What? Who says he likes me? I'm sure you're wrong about that. And anyway, I'm not mean to him," said Bean.

"Oh, Bean!" wailed Dee. "We're not wrong. He practically melts when you're around."

"He can't take his eyes off you," I said. "He totally has a crush on you!"

"It's almost disgusting, he likes you so much," Cat added. "For goodness' sake, tell him you hate him and let him transfer his affection to someone else. He's been creeping around the house morosely ever since he started helping our activity ride—and why do you think he's helping us, anyway? My other brothers tease him mercilessly. Put him out of his misery, please."

Bean looked thoughtful. "Awww, I think he's rather cute," she said, breaking into a smile.

Cat groaned.

"And if Gypsy Sylvia was right about my secret admirer, she's got to be right about me going wrong on the activity ride, doesn't she?" Bean insisted.

"You've got to get that out of your head!" Katy told her.

"I don't want to worry anyone…" Dee began. "But people are actually sitting in some of the temporary seats in the arena. You don't think all these seats are going to be filled, do you?"

We looked. All the permanent seats in the gallery were already overflowing with spectators.

"But there are hundreds of seats!" wailed Cat, looking around.

"I wish I hadn't had that hot dog now," I said, feeling really sick.

"Don't worry," said Bean, "if you feel anything like I do, one way or another you won't have it for much longer."

"You're right, Cat," said Katy grimly. "There are hundreds of seats. And that means we're going to be performing in front of hundreds of people!"

"Oh no," gulped Bean. "Maybe we should have joined the ponies in their rebellion."

Privately, I agreed with her. Watching all the expectant

faces, I was suddenly filled with an overwhelming sense of dread coupled with responsibility. What if Bean did mess up? Her track record with performances wasn't exactly impressive. This activity ride was suddenly much bigger and less fun than we had previously thought. It was serious—people had paid money to see us, and we were the finale. Looking around at the others, I could see the anxiety on their faces too.

I swallowed hard. This was turning into a pile of poo. And then things got worse.

"Pia, yoo-hoo!" shouted a familiar voice.

"Your dad's over there," said Bean, pointing. "And he's got his ultra-girly girlfriend with him."

CHAPTER 17

"Brrrr," shivered Skinny Lynny, hugging herself, "it's freezing in here. Don't they have heating in this place?"

"Not really," I sighed. "It's a riding school. They don't tend to equip riding schools with radiators."

"Well, they should," moaned Skinny. I couldn't see how she could be cold; she was wearing the biggest, puffiest down coat from her throat to her knees, sheepskin boots, big sheepskin gloves and a pair of black, fake-fur earmuffs on her head like huge ears. Usually her hair was dead straight, but today it bounced about her neck in curls. Dad had a protective arm around his trophy girlfriend. *He must have arms like an orangutan*, I thought, *for one of them to reach around that huge coat.*

"How's Drummer?" asked Dad.

I nodded. "He's great," I told him. "He's got a girlfriend. Her name's Bambi."

Skinny Lynny snickered, like humans were the only creatures who could form relationships. *With other people's dads*, I thought.

"I see your little display is on last," Dad said, waving the program at me.

"Which means we'll have to stay to the very end," Skinny sighed, sounding like she'd hoped they'd be able to watch me and run. "We haven't eaten yet," she explained.

"There's food on sale," I said. Immediately I felt stupid. Skinny Lynny eating burgers or a hot dog? That was never going to happen. An oyster bar, perhaps, or gourmet canapés, but nothing wrapped in greaseproof paper with ketchup was going to tempt her.

"Is there a bar?" Dad asked hopefully.

"I don't know, Dad," I said. "There might be one through there." I pointed to a door below the gallery.

"Let's go and find out, OK, Lyn?" Dad asked. Skinny nodded, her teeth chattering, and they disappeared.

I let out the breath I'd been holding. I found them so hard to handle.

Miraculously Bean, who had sort of melted away as soon as Dad and Skinny moved in, reappeared by my side.

"I think I'll ask for a set of earmuffs like that for Christmas," she said, looking at Skinny's retreating back. "I don't think I'll look like that in them, though."

"What, like a panda? Anyway, Declan won't mind," I told her. "You could wear one of Tiffany's old feed sacks and a saddle pad for a hat, and he'll still love you."

She gave me a shove and actually blushed. "Shut up, will you? Come on," she said. "I dare you to have your fortune told. I won't feel so bad if you do it too."

"No way!" I replied, shaking my head. "I'm too scared after your experience."

"Have you seen Alex Willard yet?" Bean asked, looking around as though he'd appear in front of her.

"No, not yet."

"I hope we do. He's so cute," Bean sighed.

"Bean, he's at least as old as my dad," I told her.

"Yes, I know, but he's still cute," she replied. I guess he was, in an ancient sort of way. We did another tour of the trade stands, and then Bean saw her mom and sisters in the crowd and said she'd better go and talk to them, seeing as they'd made the effort to come, so I looked around to see whether I could spot Mom and Mike-the-bike. *If they get here much later, they'll have to stand*, I thought. Most of the chairs had filled up, and people were leaving scarves or jackets on others to mark them as taken.

No sign of Mom. I saw James's parents—his glamorous mom was gazing intently at the silver jewelry, and his dad looked bored. I watched Sophie talking to Linda, the woman in charge of the RDA center. Sophie was pointing and Linda was nodding, no doubt they were finalizing arrangements for the ride. Mrs. Bradley and Nicky were munching on hot dogs—they gave me a wave—and I knew Leanne was around somewhere, having seen her in the crowd. I searched the sea of faces again for Alex Willard, knowing I wouldn't be able to see the demonstration of his I'd been looking forward to.

Still no sign of Alex, but I did spot Cat and Declan with a group of people I presumed to be their family—a woman, a man, another boy who looked like Cat and Dec (one of their other brothers, I thought)—and another woman with two young daughters. I did a double take. It was the same woman with the same two girls I'd seen at the yard a long time ago. The older girl had ridden Bambi. And before that, I remembered, she had turned up at the Sublime Equine Challenge and put one of the girls onto Bambi there, which had upset Cat. Looking at her now, Cat looked just as miserable. Declan was talking to the woman, but Cat was staring in the opposite direction, as though pretending not to be with the whole group, distancing herself. She looked completely desolate, like she was going to cry. *What is it about that woman?* I wondered. Every time she turned up she had the worst effect on Cat. And usually, her presence so upset her that Cat did horrible things. I hoped she wouldn't have the same effect on her today—it was bad enough with Bean convinced she was going to mess up.

That woman, I suddenly thought in a lightbulb moment, had to be somehow linked to the secret about Cat no one would tell me. I'd asked James and Bean and Katy about it, but they'd always hushed up whenever it was mentioned. It made total sense—every time this strange woman turned up, Cat went all crabby. She had to have something to do with it. But how?

I shuddered. I had a secret of my own—a two-thousand-year-old secret tucked safely in my riding pants' pocket that I hoped nobody would discover. Wasn't Cat entitled to her own secret too?

"Boo!" shouted a voice, and someone poked me in the ribs. I jumped about a mile, deep in tangled thoughts.

"I'd given up on you both!" I scolded, turning around to see Mom and Mike-the-bike grinning at me, their arms entwined like a pair of teenagers. "Didn't you come on the bike?" I asked. Rather unnecessarily, as there wasn't a leather jacket or a helmet in sight.

"Far too cold for motorcycles!" shivered Mom.

"Nah, you're just a baby," teased Mike, squeezing Mom's arm.

"We've got a program—and your name's in it!" Mom said, her eyes wide in awe.

"I know," I said.

"Well, we'll be watching you, fingers crossed!" said Mom, holding up both of her gloved hands to show me her fingers which were, indeed, crossed. Mike did the same.

"Sure you don't need it!" said Mike, winking at me.

I'd been playing the routine of the ride over in my head all day until I was sick of it. I wondered whether the hot dog I'd eaten really would put in another appearance before the night was over, my nerves were making me feel so ill.

Mom and Mike melted into the crowd. I looked back to where Cat had been, but only her family was still there. She and Dec had left them. *The strange woman looks like Cat's mom*, I thought. Only she had blond hair whereas Cat's mom was dark, like Cat.

"Aunt Pam!" I said out loud, the name popping into my

head. Declan had said something about Aunt Pam coming to watch Cat and Bambi before...before what? Cat had shut him up—in the same way Drummer had shut Tiffany up before she'd let the cat out of the bag about the pony's rebellion. What had Declan been about to let out of the bag about Cat?

I heard someone else shouting my name and turned to see Katy beckoning me to go over to her, James, and Dee. Forcing my legs in gear, I wandered over to join them. Whatever Cat's secret was involved Aunt Pam, I was sure of it now.

And I was sure that I was closer than ever to discovering what that secret was.

CHAPTER 18

I WANT YOU ALL IN your activity ride gear by the time the extravaganza starts," said Sophie bossily. "That way, we won't have to worry about lost ties and gloves. You can just tack up, mount up, warm up, and do it! Come on, get changed now. James—you can use the trailer."

Sophie's immaculate living quarters in her motor home was transformed into a frantic changing room. We all climbed into our shirts, ties, and long boots, ready for the ride. It was chaos:

"Is my tie straight?"

"Get off my jacket, Bean!"

"Oh no, I've popped a button off!"

"Ahhhh, my shirt's all wrinkled!"

"My hairnet has a hole in it!"

"Of course it does. It's a hairnet!"

"No, one big one, I mean!"

"That's where your head goes!"

"Oh ha, ha, ha, *not!*"

"Could you move from the mirror and let someone else take a look?"

"Do you know your riding pants are on backward?"

"No way! Oh, they are. I thought they felt funny."

"Anyone have a hairbrush?"

"Right, everyone stand still and let me look at you!" yelled Sophie, inspecting us like an army general surveying his troops, tucking in and smoothing down until she was satisfied.

"I can barely breathe in Leanne's jacket," said Cat, looking worried.

"Mmmm, it does look a bit tight," mused Sophie. "Do you think you'll be able to do all the movements in it?"

Cat nodded furiously, even though she looked doubtful.

"Well, you'll have to, won't you?" said Sophie. And she was right. It was too late to change things. "Didn't you think to try it on?" she asked Cat.

Cat shook her head. "I was sure it would fit," she said, sucking in her tummy.

James arrived, having changed in the trailer, and Sophie gave him the once-over too.

"You could do with a hairnet too, James," she told him. James grinned and rolled his eyes, knowing that was never going to happen.

"So do we pass inspection?" asked Katy, peering out of one of the windows. "It looks like the extravaganza is about to start, and I don't want to miss any of it."

"OK," said Sophie, satisfied. "But don't get dirty!"

We all ran to a row of seats near the door that had RESERVED on them and already held Leanne, Mrs. Bradley, Linda, and Dec. All the remaining seats were filled—which was terrifying. The arena was packed to the brim with spectators. The extravaganza was a sellout.

Sophie's friend Linda walked into the middle of the arena to give an introductory speech all about the work of the RDA and told the audience where they could get raffle tickets and refreshments and explained the program.

"I know you're all going to be thrilled by the amazing displays we have for you tonight," she said, looking tiny as she stood in the middle of the vast arena and turned to address the sea of faces. "We've got the fantastic and famous Alex Willard who will be giving a splendid display of natural horsemanship, the incredible Jive Pony—I know you're going to love seeing the ponies dancing to the music—and our finale tonight is the Laurel Farm Activity Ride, with a thrilling spectacle of daring horsemanship."

"Does she mean us?" hissed Katy.

"I feel sick," Bean said.

"That's right, give us a big buildup, and then watch their faces as the anticlimax that's our activity ride hits them!" mumbled James.

"No pressure!" groaned Cat.

I said nothing. I didn't want the others to hear my voice quivering with fright. I didn't know whether I was shivering from cold or from cold, stark fear.

"But now…" Linda continued, and whoever was working the sound system activated a recording of "Silent Night" that boomed around the arena many decibels louder than intended before adjusting it to a more acceptable level, allowing the audience to lower their hands from their ears, "we hope you'll enjoy the Taversham RDA riders' and ponies' interpretation of the Nativity, and join in the carols—the words are in the program."

The Nativity was lovely and the riders clearly all enjoyed themselves—waving to their relatives in the audience was part of the fun. The ponies were gorgeous too. From a tiny, gray pony with a forelock that reached to her nose playing the part of a sheep to a big, black-and-white pony carrying one of the wise men, they were so patient and so gentle with their riders. The helpers who were leading them clearly enjoyed themselves too. We all joined in the carol singing—forgetting our fears about the activity ride in the magic of the performance.

"Oh, that was so beautiful," sighed Bean, wiping away a tear.

"Are you all right, Bean?" asked Declan, inching closer to the object of his desire and peering intently at her face.

"Yeah, I'm fine, really," sniffed Bean, denying Declan another opportunity. "I'm just going to be the one to let everyone down, and you all have to remember to forgive me," she said dramatically.

Katy shook her head and groaned at me, and I shrugged my shoulders back at her.

"What now?" asked James, leaning over my shoulder. I knew how Declan felt. I also knew that I could never let James know just how much I liked him. How embarrassing would that be?

"Jive Pony," I told him. I'd been looking forward to this display.

Jive Pony was fantastic! A Highland pony called Ronan and his tricolored friend, Tinker, not only cantered around in circles while their riders, Rebecca and Rosie, vaulted on and off to music and did some amazing upside down stuff (and I thought hanging on to one side of Drummer while we popped over a tiny jump was impressive—it didn't even compare!), but they also did some steps to music from *Swan Lake* (with Ronan in a fluffy pink tutu) and many more amazing dances and tricks that were just incredible to watch. With Epona, as ever, in my pocket I could hear Ronan humming along to the music and scolding Rebecca whenever she was slow with the treats, and Tinker and he worked together like a couple of professional actors. Talk about cool! When Drummer and I had put a routine together for our Sublime Equine Challenge that had been hard enough even though I'd been able to talk Drummer through it—but Rebecca and Rosie didn't have an Epona to help them, which made it all the more impressive. With Jive Pony getting well-deserved thunderous applause, it was intermission time—our cue to get busy.

"Come on!" yelled Sophie, appearing out of nowhere to hurry us along. "Let's get going!"

As I got up, I caught sight of Mom and Mike-the-bike in the front row, and they both gave me the thumbs-up sign, accompanied by silly grins. I managed a half grin back in their direction.

"Who are those crazy people up there waving?" Cat asked no one in particular, pulling a disgusted face as she looked up toward the part of the gallery with a glass front.

I followed her gaze and saw Dad and Skinny Lynny jump-ing up and down. They'd found the bar. *Maybe they'll be tipsy enough not to notice any mistakes*, I thought. That would be a good thing. I really wished I hadn't eaten that hot dog. Huge mistake—right from the start. How dumb was I? Ugh!

Drummer was as cool as a cucumber and shared none of my anxieties.

"Is it our turn?" he asked, munching from his hay net. Pulling half-eaten, chewed-on bits of hay out of his mouth, I put his bridle on, my hands shaking.

"Oh, be careful. That was my eye!" he grumbled. "What's the matter with your hands?"

"I'm terrified!" I told him. "You won't believe the num-ber of people out there waiting to notice the slightest mis-take any of us makes."

"Get a grip!" Drummer snapped. "We've done the rou-tine millions of times. You must know it by now!"

"I know, I know, it's all going on in my head, over and over again. I know it by heart. It's just so scary doing it in front of so many people. What were we thinking? I mean, Bean's convinced she's going to mess up, and if she messes up, we all will. It could be a disaster!"

"They'll love it," Drummer assured me. "And Bean's right at the back, so she only has to copy everyone else. Honestly, why are you so nervous? You know the routine by heart, you know you do!"

"What's up?" I heard Bambi ask Drummer as I led him down the ramp to join her in the parking lot.

"She's got cold feet," explained Drummer. "What would you do with them, eh?"

"Don't ask me," Bambi replied, yawning. "Cat's just told me she's scared to death she'll ruin it for everyone. What were the practices for?"

"Search me!" Drummer replied.

I looked across at Cat. She looked back at me.

"I'm terrified we'll mess everything up," I told her, expecting her to poo-poo my lack of confidence.

Cat grinned at me. "Yeah, me too," she said.

It was the first time we'd agreed on anything.

"You'll be great," I offered, sensing an opportunity. "You and Bambi are awesome leaders."

"I hope you're right," Cat said grimly, pulling down her stirrups, "because we all have to be pretty amazing tonight."

Mounting Drummer, I headed for the warm-up arena—an outside school adjacent to the big arena. The others were already riding around, and James was being extra firm with Henry who had virtually given up trying to wreck the ride, realizing that he only had to get through tonight and he could go back to being his usual horrible, uncooperative self with the soft-touch owner.

Our helpers were all dressed in black trousers and gray sweatshirts that Sophie had gotten for them, and they looked pretty cool. I hardly recognized Declan—apart from his hair, of course. He looked embarrassed because he was so clean-cut.

A few well-wishing parents gathered around the entrance

as we trotted and cantered around, and Sophie yelled a few helpful comments such as, "Bambi's over-bent. Cat, loosen your grip a little," and "Bean, shorten your reins. They're like washing lines," and "Dee, don't let Dolly dawdle like that—she's hardly moving! Your ponies all need to be listening to you and responsive to your every command!"

"Jeez, she's wound up like an eight-day clock!" muttered Drummer.

"Yeah, like we don't know what's expected of us," replied Bambi. "You'd think we had nothing to do with it and it was all down to the humans, heaven forbid!"

I concentrated on getting Drummer warm, without tiring him—he had a lot to do in the next ten minutes. It was freezing, and he kept trying to buck, which didn't help things. I ran the routine in my head three whole times and sighed. Drum was right. I knew it off by heart, thank goodness!

We could hear the Alex Willard demonstration in full swing—Alex had a microphone to help him explain to the audience what he was doing. I had hoped I'd bump into him outside, but our paths hadn't crossed. Gazing wistfully toward the doors, I wished I could be inside watching his fantastic and empathetic way with horses. It was something I never tired of watching. His announcement that he was starting on his final demonstration was Sophie's cue for the final countdown.

"OK, come over here one at a time to get your cloths on your ponies' front legs," she told us. "Leanne, you're really good at this. Can you do Tiffany while I start on Dolly? And once your cloths are on, everyone, I don't want you splashing around in the outdoor school getting them dirty. Throw a rug over your pony's quarters and walk them around on the concrete to keep them warm," she instructed us, bending down to clothe Dolly by the glow of the floodlights. With Henry and Bluey clothed as well, there was only Bambi and Drummer to do last. Drummer stood like a rock while Sophie bent down and wrapped his legs in green crepe, and Leanne did the honors for Bambi.

"You look great," I heard Drummer tell Bambi. Bambi fluttered her eyelashes back at him and told him he looked very handsome. *They really are in love*, I thought.

"OK," said Sophie, straightening up, "that's it. You all look very professional."

We lined up in front of our trainer, our four helpers included, for a final inspection.

"You all know the routine," Sophie said, eyeing us up and down. "Everyone knows what they have to do, so just go out there and enjoy yourselves!"

Was she joking?

"I don't think I can remember anything," said Bean, shakily. Sophie frowned at her and snapped, "Don't start that nonsense, Bean. Of course you remember—once you get in there, it will all come back to you."

No one mentioned Gypsy Sylvia. Sophie would have gone insane if she'd known about Bean's jaunt with fortune-telling. Closing my eyes, I played the routine again in my head. Left, right, pairs, two rides, line of jumps, arms outstretched, jackets off, jackets on, over onto one stirrup, pairs, broom handles in a diamond, broom handles in a cross, broom handles all abreast, line up for the backward roll dismount—it was all in there, waiting to be ridden out in the arena. I took a deep breath, letting it out slowly in an effort to calm myself. It seemed to help.

We made our way to the entrance, and if I craned my neck, I could make out Alex Willard answering questions from the audience.

"He can take as long as he wants to do that," James said miserably. "I'm in no hurry to make a fool of myself in front of these people."

"Do you feel as nervous as I do?" I asked him.

"I dunno, how nervous do you feel?" he asked me, grinning. "Anyway," he continued, "in about ten minutes it will all be over."

"We are so going to give a fantastic performance," said Katy, stroking Bluey's neck. She was always the upbeat one, always the one to see a positive when everyone else could see only negatives. I took a deep breath.

"You're right, Katy!" I said, psyching myself up even more, the routine buzzing in my mind as I fast-forwarded the whole ride. "We're the best activity ride this audience will ever see!"

"Yeah, well, I don't think they've seen very many, so that's not hard to do," I heard Drummer say to Bambi.

I patted his neck. "I'm so up for this, Drum. We're going to be fantastic!"

"I hope so," said Cat, overhearing me, "because we're on. Linda's giving us the big buildup now. According to her, we're the best thing since, since…"

"Alex Willard?" joked James.

And then, miraculously, Alex Willard himself was walking out of the arena past me. Only he didn't go past. He recognized me and came over, instead.

"Pia? It is you! I was hoping I'd see you."

Everyone else just stared. "Er, hi!" I mumbled, thrilled and embarrassed, still running the ride routine through my head.

"I'm looking forward to your activity ride," Alex continued, his eyes sparkling, his gray hair silver in the moonlight. "I'll be watching from here. Good luck!"

I heard our intro music, and as Sophie ran down behind us pulling the rugs off the ponies, our helpers walked into the arena to take their positions.

I heard Cat whisper *wow* as Alex melted into the background.

"OK," Sophie shouted as Cat edged Bambi in front, ready for the start, "you know what you have to do. Go knock 'em dead out there!"

Nudging Drummer into a trot behind Bambi, we burst into the brightly lit arena, a sea of faces surrounding us, giving us a thunderous round of applause. I wondered whether Tiffany was freaking out behind me, but there was nowhere to hide—this was our big moment. We were stars, and now we had to discover whether we could live up to our big buildup. I felt myself grinning as we lined up—so this was showbiz!

Staring at Drummer's glossy black mane stretching out in front of me, I felt my grin evaporate as my mind went suddenly, totally blank. Seeing Alex Willard had done something terrible to my memory banks, and I suddenly realized in one heart-stopping, breathless moment that it was me, not Bean, who was going to let the whole ride down. Because I couldn't remember a single movement of the activity ride we'd practiced and practiced for weeks. I couldn't remember anything at all.

Chapter 19

"Drummer," I whispered as we bobbed along behind Bambi, "Drummer, I've forgotten it."

"What?" Drummer yelled. There was no need for him to whisper.

"The routine. It's gone. Help me!"

I heard Drummer groan. *That's supportive*, I thought.

"OK, I've got you covered," he added. "But try as hard as you can to remember and let me know when it comes back to you."

"What makes you think it will come back to me?" I hissed.

"We're splitting up here, go left…of course it will come back to you. It *will*! Now we're making pairs so we need to get level with Bambi."

I looked across the arena and steadied Drum so that we met at the bottom in line with Cat.

"You look like you're about to throw up," Cat hissed at me.

"I can't remember a single thing!" I hissed back. Immediately, I regretted telling her. Cat was bound to let me mess up. I froze even more at the thought. I had underestimated her.

"It's diagonals next," Cat told me anxiously, "across the center."

Of course, I thought. *Yes, diagonals*. Cat was right. And what was more, she wasn't going to let me ruin the whole ride. I felt my shoulders dropping slightly as I relaxed for a microsecond, secure in my next movement. As we flew past behind Cat, I saw her turn and mouth the words "two rides next" at me. The next movement! I had to be the leader of a ride of three. Oh no, what did I do then? Luckily, Drummer took control.

"You just sit there," I heard him muttering sarcastically. "Just rest a little and let me handle this."

And I did. I couldn't help it. *Thank goodness for Epona*, I thought, knowing my little stone statue was safely tucked into my riding pants' pocket. Without her I wouldn't be able to hear Drummer, and I'd never know he was helping me. How did other people get on without a two-thousand-year-old goddess to look after them?

We got through the two rides movement, and then our helpers ran in with the jumps while we rode around the outside. I caught sight of Cat's anxious face scanning mine, and I managed a grin at her when I realized that I knew what to do next—and after that, and after that. The activity ride had come back to me with a whoosh, and I heaved a huge sigh of relief. Thank goodness!

With the routine back in my head, I started to enjoy myself. The crowd cheered enthusiastically as we stripped off our jackets over the jumps. They clapped as we put them on again, and they cheered even louder when we tackled the jumps on one stirrup without a single mistake. It was like being movie stars or something, and it was obvious that everyone else, including Bean, was remembering the routine and doing really well. When our helpers got into position with the broom handles, I could hear the audience gasp with amazement as we flew over the narrow jumps, missing the helpers by the smallest of margins (Mrs. B. had her eyes shut for most of the time, I noticed). It really was thrilling—Sophie had put together a fantastic routine that was enthralling to watch, and I half wished I could see it. I hoped someone was recording it so I could see it later.

When everyone jumped the handles abreast, I glanced sideways at James on Henry, who winked at me as all the ponies took off at exactly the same stride—just how we were supposed to. *Phew*, I thought, *we are almost done!*

Lining up, the audience thought it was all over, and when Cat started her backward roll off Bambi and we all followed in succession, I heard more amazed gasps, followed by a huge round of applause and cheering.

"Wow!" I heard Bean say. "We were a pretty good finale after all!"

"That's the biggest cheer of the night!" Drummer puffed proudly. The ponies hadn't been worried at all about the audience—I could hear Dolly gushing about having such a big crowd. She loved it.

I messed up Drummer's mane a bit and told him he was the best pony in the whole world, a title he accepted without question—of course. I meant it too.

As our helpers and Sophie joined us in a bow, we all

mounted up for our exit from the arena. Glancing sideways, my eyes met with Cat's.

"Thanks for helping me," I said.

Cat grinned back at me. "Anytime," she replied.

Chapter 20

"YOU WERE ALL, *ALL*, *terrific*!" Sophie cheered as we came to a jumbled halt outside the arena. Fired up, we were all laughing and beaming from the euphoria of completing the ride without a mistake and excited by the enthusiastic reaction of the crowd. It had gone better than anyone had thought—especially Bean.

"Phew," she sighed, sliding out of Tiffany's saddle and landing on the concrete. "I'm so glad I didn't mess up. That Sylvia woman was wrong!"

"That was so good! And so were you, Henry," said James, thumping Henry's neck. He quit both stirrups and threw his right leg over Henry's neck, sliding to the ground in a forbidden dismount, taking his hat off at the same time, and running his fingers through his long, blond hair. Sophie threw him a look but let it slide. Mrs. Bradley, however, didn't know who to hug first.

"Oh, James, oh, Henry, you were both wonderful!" she cried. No, literally, she did cry—I could see tears in her eyes as she praised them both. "Thank you, James," she added, her hand on his arm, "my Henry has never done anything so clever—and he never will again, not with me. You can ride him whenever you want to."

"You are joking!" I heard Henry snort in dismay.

James put his arm around her shoulders and gave her a hug. "Thanks, Mrs. B.," he said. "You were a saint to lend me Henry, and you were pretty talented with the broom handles too!"

Mrs. Bradley blushed. How cute! I thought it would serve Henry right if James did take Mrs. B. up on her offer to ride him. I couldn't see him volunteering unless desperate, though. I knew he couldn't wait for Moth to be healthy again.

Bean's mom and sisters arrived and were actually enthusiastic about her riding. That was a first. Bean looked shocked—and Tiffany started doing little half rears when Bean's arty sisters got too close, causing them to back off again in fright.

And then Cat's family appeared out of nowhere, including her Aunt Pam with her two daughters—both of whom were breathless and excited. Aunt Pam lifted the younger one to stroke Bambi's face. I could hear Bambi and Drummer talking to each other about the ride and one-upping each other for a job well done—they took no notice of the human family gathering. In the instant her aunt arrived, the euphoria Cat had expressed was wiped from her face, and she sat mutely on Bambi's back, staring into space. Aunt Pam filled the void.

"That was fantastic, Catriona," I overheard her say, returning her youngest daughter to the ground and thumping Bambi's two-tone neck. "You've really fired the girls up, hasn't she, girls? They're dying to ride her more now they've seen her in action. Emily wants to do exactly what her cousin Catriona has done on my Bam-Bam." The eldest of her daughters reached up to stroke Bambi's nose, and the younger one jumped up and down in excitement.

Bam-Bam, I thought. Cat hates Bambi being called Bam-Bam. Was that why she was looking like thunder?

"The girls can't wait to have her back," Aunt Pam continued, "and I have to say that after seeing that, I can't either. The start of summer vacation will be perfect. Emily's old enough to ride by herself now and our pasture at home is just as she left it. I may even get back into it myself. We'll say the middle of July. That's settled."

Who is Aunt Pam having back, I wondered, *and what pasture is she talking about?*

Glancing at Cat, I was horrified to see that she looked close to tears. Surely it was OK for Aunt Pam's kids to ride Bambi in the summer? I'd seen them ride her before at the yard—Cat had led them around herself. My thoughts were interrupted by a shout in my direction as I dismounted and hugged Drum.

"Hey, Pia, showbiz riding star!" yelled a voice. It was Mike-the-bike, my mom in tow. They had both been ultra-impressed with our performance.

"Although if I'd known half the things you were going to do on that activity ride, I'd never have signed the consent form," Mom scolded. "Hanging over one side of Drummer indeed—hi, Drummer, you clever boy, have a sugar cube—while you went over jumps, not to mention that somersault you did at the end. Terrifying!"

"I thought the routines over the jumps were amazing," Mike said, patting Drummer's neck. Drummer crunched the sugar cubes Mom gave him and frisked her pockets for more. "You're an Evel Knievel on a horse, aren't you?"

"Who?" I asked.

"Never mind," said Mike, rolling his eyes at my ignorance.

"Hey, Pia!" It was Alex Willard again. I remembered the last time he'd met my mom. Not good! Little did I know that this time would be just as memorable—for a different reason.

"Congratulations! That was just incredible!" Alex told me, patting Drummer. "Hello," he said, holding out his hand to my mom and giving her a devastating smile. "I'm Alex Willard."

"Yes, I remember," my mom replied coolly. She smiled and shook his hand.

Alex Willard did a double take. "Er, Sue, isn't it?"

Mom nodded.

The last time they'd met, my mom had been tipsy and had embarrassed me by flirting with Alex. Alex had fled. This time, it seemed things were different. Alex Willard liked my mom—it was obvious! And looking at my mom through Alex Willard's eyes, I could see why. She was looking great! All bouncy curls and long eyelashes, oozing with confidence. She was a million miles away from the desperate and tired woman who had cornered him at the TV studios.

My mom introduced Mike, but it didn't make much

difference to Alex—he kept gazing at my mom like Declan did at Bean. It was weird! Mike seemed very cool about it. So cool, the thought bounced into my head, that he might not care too much. This was followed immediately by lots more thoughts—all involving Alex Willard and my mom. It felt as though my head would explode.

"Come on, mount up!" Sophie shouted, interrupting my galloping mind. "Everyone in the extravaganza is required to do a lap of honor before Linda winds up the show. I want you to ride in your pairs, so make sure you keep together."

We scrambled back onto our mounts—Henry complaining that he had thought his role was over. He was just told to shut up and get on with it by the others.

All the extravaganza acts returned to rapturous applause—and we got the biggest cheer of all. It was like being a total star. Drum and Bambi cantered around, their strides perfectly matched, but Cat said nothing. Glancing across at her, I was astonished to see that she looked totally miserable—unlike the rest of us who were on a bit of a high with all the clapping and cheering we could hear. I had been right about her Aunt Pam; she had the most awful effect on her, and she had to be part of the big secret. Galloping out again, we pulled up and walked to the motor home and trailer. The extravaganza was all over. I was still on a high when I tied Drummer up to the side of Sophie's motor home next to Bambi so I could take off his tack and rug him up. I told him how wonderful he was. Naturally, he didn't deny it or make any pretense at modesty. Instead, he took all the credit.

"So," he said, attacking the hay net like he was starved, "how good were we tonight?"

"We were perfect!" I told him. "You were right. It did all come back to me, thank goodness!"

"Not you," Drummer said. "Us. The ponies. How totally amazing were we?"

I smiled. "Yes," I told him, "you all totally rocked. Thanks!"

"Oh, don't mention it," Drum replied. "It was nothing."

Yeah, I thought, *right!*

"What's up with Cat?" asked James, appearing at my side.

"What do you mean?" I said, looking around. Bambi was rugged up, but her owner had fled.

"She's around the other side being comforted by Katy and Dee. She's crying her eyes out. Don't tell me she's overcome with the emotion of our performance."

"What's going on?" said Bean, joining us.

"Something's up with Cat," James explained. "Very upset—like mega tears."

"Oh, it's probably"—Bean glanced at James—"you know, her Aunt Pam's been creeping around."

"What is it about Aunt Pam?" I asked them both. "Come on, you've stayed quiet about whatever it is Cat gets upset about for long enough. I know there's a big secret. I heard Aunt Pam tell Cat that the pasture was all ready, and the summer vacation would be the perfect time. The perfect time for what? What's the big deal?"

James and Bean exchanged glances. James looked at me in a resigned way. "We might as well tell you. It sounds like you'll know soon enough, anyway."

"It's Bambi," Bean said, gulping. "She doesn't actually belong to Cat, she belongs to her Aunt Pam…"

"She loaned her to Cat while she had her two kids, and Cat only has Bambi for as long as it's OK with her aunt," continued James.

"And now," I said, understanding Cat's secret at last and the reason why she was so upset, "Aunt Pam wants her back."

"Yup," James said, nodding. "And there's nothing Cat can do about it!"

CHAPTER 21

DRUMMER WAS DISTRAUGHT.

"Do you know that Bambi's leaving?" he stared at me in disbelief.

I nodded glumly, thinking how different everything suddenly was. Before our activity ride, if someone had told me that Cat and Bambi were going, I'd have been relieved to learn that I only had to wait until next summer until I could look forward to a Cat-free yard, when she would no longer have the opportunity to mock me and make things unpleasant. But since the ride, well, things had changed. And, of course, Drummer and Bambi were such an item now, and I could only imagine how he must be feeling. It had taken him such a long time to win her around, and now he faced losing her.

"Does Bambi know?" I asked him.

"She told me. She's really upset. She says she used to live with this Pam woman before and didn't like it. She has a stable in her back yard, and a pasture, and there's only room for one pony, so she didn't have any company. She was really lonely, and next summer—next summer—she's going to have to go back there. Alone. Bambi doesn't want to go back. She likes it here with us, with me!"

Sticking his head over his stable door, Drummer stared unseeing across the yard to where Dolly and Tiffany were chatting over their half-doors. "She can't go," he murmured. "We're a team. We all get along and besides…" He gulped, unable to go on.

I leaned against his shoulder and felt Drum's rough mane against my cheek. "Bambi belongs to Cat's aunt. Being with Cat was only a temporary arrangement," I explained.

"Why didn't you tell me this before?"

"I didn't know. It's the big secret no one would tell me, remember?"

Drummer turned his head. "Oh, that. It's just as well we didn't know sooner—I'd have had more time to be miserable."

I let myself out of the door and walked over to the tack room feeling really down. I hadn't seen Cat since the evening of the extravaganza and tonight was Christmas Eve. *What a Christmas present*, I thought, knowing she only had a matter of months with Bambi. I knew she'd be at the yard soon to make Bambi comfortable for the night. Dusk was falling, and the air all around was cold and still. James was in the tack room, rummaging around in Moth's tack box.

"How's Drummer?" he asked.

I sighed. "There's nothing I can say to console him. How can Cat bear it? I can't imagine how I would feel if Drummer was going to be whisked away from me. It's just awful."

"You two have never gotten along," James reminded me.

"So what?" I said. "This is something I wouldn't wish upon my worst enemy, and besides, Drum loves Bambi, and I can't bear to see him so upset. If only there was something we could do!" I couldn't believe how different things were now. I was with Cat on this one—it was a total turnaround.

Katy walked in with Bluey's tack and heaved it onto her saddle rack. "What are you two looking so sad about?" she asked.

"Bambi," we chorused.

"Oh," Katy said, frowning.

"There has to be something we can do!" I repeated.

"Like what?" Katy asked, throwing her hat into her tack box and shaking her red hair loose from a band. Silence filled the tack room. The air was thick with lack of inspiration. I had to do something for Drummer's sake. I couldn't, I wouldn't, let him down. I felt my hands clenching into fists by my sides and my heart pounding in my chest. "We can't just do nothing," I said. "We can't just sit back and watch Bambi go. We have to make sure Cat keeps her."

"How can we?" said Katy.

"I don't know," I replied, "but I know we have to try. Will you help me?"

"Yes, count me in!" James said firmly.

"Definitely!" Katy said, nodding frantically. "And you know Bean and Dee will help too."

"OK then," I said determinedly. "The Keep Bambi Campaign starts right here. We're not going to let her go!"

Coming soon...

The Pony Whisperer

STABLES SOS!

CHAPTER 1

I LAY IN THE SUNSHINE and racked my brains. At last we had time to think. But then, just as we found some time to give the problem our full attention, yet another diversion arrived. Only today, relaxing in the field, we didn't know just how big a diversion it was going to be.

"Uh-oh, look out, two more lost souls," remarked Katy, twirling a blade of grass around her mouth and squinting against the sunlight. Lazily, I turned and followed her gaze, frowning as my eyes found their target. It was a man and a woman, standing in the ponies' field, looking around and pointing.

"Go and tell them to clear off," murmured James rudely. "Honestly, some hikers think they can just walk anywhere—including our ponies' field. And they're ruining my concentration," he added.

"They don't look much like hikers," mused Katy. "They're both wearing suits. Who hikes in a suit?"

"Who cares?" mumbled Bean. "Is there any more candy, Pia?"

"Nope, all gone," I told her, putting the last piece in my mouth and chewing. I refused to be distracted. *How awful we are at inspiration*, I thought, still planless. Total, complete, garbage. Time was ticking away, and we still had nothing. Nada. Zilch. Big, fat zero. Frankly, my head hurt.

"They must be hikers," sighed James, shielding his eyes against the sun as he looked across the field, "because they're looking at a map."

"They're freaking Tiffany out," Bean said huffily.

I looked over to where Tiffany had been grazing with Katy's blue roan gelding Bluey and James's chestnut mare Moth. Bean's palomino mare was doing her best giraffe impersonation, head high, eyes out on stalks, staring at the two strangers in dismay. You'd think they were a couple of yeti, not just an ordinary man and a woman. The trouble with Tiffany is that she's unnerved by anything out of the ordinary. And, I have to say, quite a lot of things in the ordinary too.

"Everything scares Tiffany," James snorted.

"She's really brave!" Bean protested indignantly.

"What?" asked Katy, bewildered.

"Explain!" I demanded.

"OK, so she is scared of everything, but she still goes past things for me, things your ponies aren't scared of," Bean said. "It's easy for your ponies, but Tiffany has to face her fears every day. That makes her extra brave."

"One hundred percent Bean logic," Katy sighed, lying back down in the grass and gazing up at the sky.

"I wonder how Dee's doing," I said. She had gone to a show with her pony, Dolly Daydream. I imagined them cantering around the ring looking fabulous, accepting a red rosette, posing for photographers from the horsey press. The type of show Dee entered would have those. Horsey press photographers didn't bother going to shows attended by the likes of Drummer and me.

"Mmmm, I wonder how poor old Mrs. Collins is doing," said Katy, looking through her red candy wrapper at Bluey. "Oh, wow, Bluey looks fabulous as a strawberry roan. But then, he would," she added, totally besotted by her pony.

"Yeah, poor Mrs. C.," agreed Bean.

Mrs. Collins was our ponies' landlady and, as I've mentioned, she lived alone in her house on the yard. Except that she wasn't living there at the moment because only a week ago she'd been carted off to hospital in an ambulance after suffering a heart attack. Sophie, Dee-Dee's mom, was looking after Mrs. Collins's cats and greyhound, Swish, and we were all pitching in, glad to help. Old Mrs. C. was a bit crazy, but everyone was hoping she'd be back soon. I mean, she was OK really, and sometimes, almost sane.

"I think you should tell those two trespassers to go away, James," said Katy bossily.

"Well, it's strange, but they don't look very lost," James replied. "They look like they mean to be here. You go and tell them if you're that worried."

"I'm too comfortable," Katy snorted, "and you're being such a wimp! Here, Bean." She waved the candy wrapper in Bean's direction. "See what Tiffany looks like pink."

"No thanks. I like her all golden and gorgeous. I'll go

and tell them," Bean volunteered, getting to her feet and stretching. Nearby, Drummer and Bambi lifted their heads from grazing, still chewing as they watched Bean walk across the field toward the gate where the two strangers were standing.

I could imagine the conversation: Bean would politely ask them whether they were lost. They would nod their heads and ask where the footpath was. Bean would point to the next field. They would thank her and head for the right path, avoiding the pony poo and climbing through the fence, turning to give Bean a wave of thanks. It happened now and again. I'd given directions to people who had gotten lost on a walk before.

My gaze swung around to Drummer. He really is the most wonderful, fabulous bay pony. OK, he isn't the most polite pony in the world (sometimes he's downright rude), but he has a heart of gold, even if he does hide it successfully. And there was Bambi standing next to him, as close as she could get, her muzzle resting on Drummer's mahogany back. I heard myself sigh. If we didn't come up with some sort of plan soon…

"There must be a way!" Katy said, as though able to hear my thoughts. She said it at least once a day. She'd been saying it at least once a day since Santa's busiest night of the year.

"Yes, there must," James agreed, exasperated, "but the trouble is, we don't know what it is!"

"Yet!" I said, determined to be positive.

"Let's go through it again…" began Katy. James groaned, and my heart sank too. We didn't need to spell it out again. We knew what we had to do. We just didn't know how to do it.

"There has to be a way!" Katy said again, scratching her head, determined that if she said it enough times, the answer would present itself to her. It hadn't yet. Her red hair was caught back in a band—purple of course. She never seemed to wear any other color. James had once asked her, in mock seriousness, whether she thought she would grow out of purple and graduate to, say, green or blue. Katy had just stared at him as though he was insane.

"Yes, there is a way, Katy," James said. "We're just waiting for you to tell us what it is. So what is it?"

Katy screwed up her candy wrapper and threw it at James.

"Ahhhh!" screamed James dramatically, his hand flying upward and covering one side of his face. "My eye, my eye!"

For a second, Katy looked appalled, then realizing she'd been tricked, she gave James a shove. "Very funny!" she said. "*Not!*" she added.

Bean hurried back across the field. She looked a lot less relaxed than she had when she'd left us. Something wasn't right. I looked over to the gate. The man and the woman were still there, looking around them and writing something down in a notebook.

"What's up?" asked James, noticing Bean's expression. She flopped down beside us and tore at the grass, her eyebrows knotting together in a frown under her blond bangs. "Weren't they grateful to be shown the right path?"

"They're not hikers," said Bean, chewing her lip.

"Then why were they looking at a map?" asked Katy.

"It wasn't a map," gulped Bean.

"Who are they then?" I asked.

"The man said his name was Robert Collins. He said he was Mrs. Collins's son."

"I didn't know she had any family," said Katy, sitting up. "She never said."

We stared at the strangers with renewed interest, fixating on the man, the Robert Collins one, the Mrs. Collins's son one.

"I've never seen him before," added James.

"Well, that's what he said," Bean said, shrugging her shoulders. Her voice was all wobbly.

"So what's he doing here? Now?" Katy asked her.

Bean sniffed. James edged closer and put his arm around her shoulders, sparking pangs of jealousy in my heart. I only hoped James would never find out about my unrequited feelings for him.

"What is it, Bean? Why are you so upset? What did they say to you?" he asked gently.

"They said…" began Bean. "Robert Collins said…" She stopped.

I felt my heart skip a beat for a different reason. Whatever had Mrs. Collins's son said to upset Bean so much?

Bean gulped. "He told me that he was selling Laurel

Farm for development." Bean started crying. "The paper was covered in plans for new houses in this very field, and he said that we would all have to find new homes for the ponies!"

ABOUT THE AUTHOR

Janet Rising's work with horses has included working at a donkey stud, producing show ponies, and teaching both adults and children, with a special interest in helping nervous riders enjoy their sport, as well as training owners on how to handle their horses and ponies from the ground. Always passionate about writing, Janet's first short story was published when she was fourteen, and for the past ten years, she has been editor of *PONY*, Britain's top-selling horsy teen magazine.